OLD LOVE

Old Love

➤

MARGARET ERHART

For Cathy:

oct 93

Best Margaret erhart

STEERFORTH PRESS

South Royalton, Vermont

For information about permission to reproduce selections
from this book, write to: Steerforth Press L.C., P.O. Box 70,
South Royalton, Vermont 05068.

A part of this book originally appeared as the short story "Tommie" in the
Paradise Lost issue of the *Global City Review.*

Library of Congress Cataloging-in-Publication Data
Erhart, Margaret
Old Love : a novel / Margaret Erhart.
p.   cm.
ISBN 1–883642–73–6
1. Family—New Jersey—Fiction.   I. Title.
PS3555.R426043   1996
813'.54—dc20   95-48320 CIP

Manufactured in the United States of America

FIRST PAPERBACK EDITION

PART ONE

Helen

Before we lived next door to Hal, we lived in a house I barely remember. I think it was yellow. The walls of my room were light blue. In bed I would run the back of my hand up and down the wall, up and down the rough, cool plaster. That was the only way I could go to sleep. My door had a glass doorknob. I liked to turn it with both hands. It too was cool, and faceted like a diamond. When I cried, it helped to press my forehead against it.

Tommie, my mother, was my best friend then. This was before I went to school. My older brother, Brighton, was my friend in the afternoon and on weekends. Dad I hardly knew.

There was a deer path that led from our house to a pond called Callus Pond. In the spring we walked through a skunk cabbage bog to get there, holding our noses. Tommie took us there in the winter. She carried my double-runner skates and a thermos of hot chocolate. Brighty carried his own skates. He had hockey skates. All the boys did. Whenever he met some of his friends at the pond, he pretended not to know us.

I'd watch him go out into the middle, his ankles soft as putty, bowing in, his jacket flapping, his long scarf falling off him, trailing on the ice. Some kind of love or sorrow compelled me, and I'd leave the shore and Tommie to follow him.

"Brighty! Brighty!"

"Go away, Helen. Go back."

"Wait! I'm coming with you."

"You can't. Mom, call her."

"Why can't I? I can keep up."

"They're not your friends. They're my friends."

"I'll just be with you."

"I don't want you to."

He'd wobble away, dropping a mitten or the hat off his head, and I'd skate back to Tommie. The cure for a broken heart was hot chocolate. When it got cold or dark enough, we'd go home.

When Brighton was eight he fell through the ice on Callus Pond. An older boy named John Hammond dared him and he pointed his skates right for the middle, three days into the January thaw. He didn't get far. It wasn't deep. He didn't die and come back again. He went in up to his waist. He wasn't drowning. All the air in our corner of New Jersey was his to breathe. And the day was mild, the water beneath the ice sluggish and brown, thick with slimy grasses. His skates cut into the soft mud at the bottom of the pond. The ragged ice surrounded him like a tutu. At first he looked neither cold nor desperate — just bewildered. He tried to raise himself, but each time he lifted his soggy weight the ice around him gave way. Finally he started to cry. Only a minute had passed — it all happened so quickly. I was just five years old but I knew right then it was loneliness that might kill him, a boy alone in the middle of what looked like a giant, frozen costume.

We were twenty yards from him on solid ground, Tommie and John Hammond's father and I, hurrying along the shore to get as close to him as possible before John's father would slide out to him on his belly, pushing a tree limb ahead of him. Suddenly Brighton screamed and shot up, actually launched himself out of the hole.

John Hammond's father yelled, "Whoa! You all right?"

"We're coming, we're coming, we're coming," I whispered, and crossed my fingers.

"What happened?" called Tommie. "Brighton?"

He scrabbled like a dog to keep from sliding back into the water. Then he lay on his belly, exhausted, and sobbed, "A fish touched my hand."

John's father shouted instructions and soon he swam over to us on top of the ice. His skates left a crazy design, like a car out of control. The ice was soft and a ridge of slush built up across his chest as he came. He looked determined and sad. His hat sat on the very top of his head and his hair stuck out wildly. He was pale, even with the exertion. He dragged across the ice like a moth in candle wax, his arms fluttering an airy breaststroke against his body's heavy, rocking weight.

On the way home I asked if we ever had to go to the pond again. "Of course we do," said Tommie. Brighton walked beside her, wrapped in John Hammond's father's coat. John's father had offered to drive us home but Tommie said no, it wasn't far, it was right up the hill. We would walk. We would warm up walking. I waited for Brighton to say he wouldn't get in the car with John Hammond anyway, but he didn't say it. So I said it, and Tommie told me not to be rude. He said nothing all the way home, and almost nothing for the next ten years.

That summer we moved next door to Hal. He was Tommie's friend. She had known him in college when he was thin and funny and had a thousand friends. The Hal I met was chubby and lived alone in a big brick house with a swimming pool. On weekends he had parties. His friends came out from the city and filled the field between our two houses with their cars. In summer they played softball and swam in the pool, and in the evening stood around the pool drinking and eating catered hors d'oeuvres. The whole house was lit up all night long, and from my window I could see couples dancing in Hal's high-ceilinged living room, or outside on the veranda. Once I saw two men stripped to the waist, boxing in his bedroom.

We went over to meet Hal during the day. I remember it was broad, hot daylight. We were going to go over the night before, when we first got there. Tommie couldn't wait to go. We hadn't even set our suitcases down when she said, "Let's go say hi next door. Helen? Brighty? Frank, do you want to come?" But Brighton didn't want to go if it was dark out, and I didn't want to go if he didn't go, and Dad said, "You go, Tommie. I'll put the kids to bed. Go."

In the morning we ate a good breakfast and I put my swimsuit on under my shorts in case he invited us to use his pool. Dad said he had work to do, which meant he'd sit and read the paper. Tommie took the two of us over. We walked across the field, one of us on each side of her. She knocked — she never used a doorbell. Hal opened the door and he was plump, something I'd never noticed before in a man. It made me suspicious of him. He was wearing green Bermuda shorts and a pink, short-sleeved Oxford shirt with a ragged collar. His hair was blond and thin. He looked like Captain Kangaroo on television, with a jowly but friendly face. When he kissed Tommie right on the lips I looked at the floor. Brighty did too. It was carpeted, something I wasn't used to. Hal was barefoot and I remember he wore a thin gold chain around one ankle.

Dad had told us to call him Mr. Chapin, to call all adults Mr. or Mrs. or Miss. After the kiss, Tommie pushed me forward with a little pressure on my shoulder. Even though I was younger, I always went first in these cases to give Brighty a sense of what to do or say. Tommie said, "Can you look at people when you speak, Helen?" I looked at Hal's knees. "What do you say? Can you say hello?"

"Hello."

"Hello who?"

"Hello, Mr. Chapin."

"Hi," said Hal. It was clear he didn't know what to do with children. Children have radar for this kind of thing. He started to bend over, then decided against it and straightened up again and got down on one knee. It was the strangest thing I'd ever seen a grown-up do that involved me. He had a mole right under his left eye and he smelled of coffee. "Helen?" he said. "You're Helen, right?"

"Uh-huh."

"Well, Mr. Chapin . . . that's my father's name. You better call me Hal."

We swam that day, almost all day, Hal and I did. In a bathing suit he looked like a woman. He had breasts. He had a roll of flesh around his middle, and his thighs stuck to each other. His bottom went up and down when he walked. But in the water he turned into a seal. A great big seal. A walrus. Tommie watched while I paddled around in the shallow end. Hal dove and surfaced and floated on his back, or cannonballed off the diving board. Brighton hated to swim. He sat and shivered at the edge of the pool, whining at Tommie to take him home. Hal called him Brighty Boy. "How can you be cold, Brighty Boy? It's summertime. See this?" Another cannonball. "I can teach you that if you want. You want to learn it?" I don't think Brighton said more than two words to him that day. The name Brighty Boy was Hal's first mistake. The next was to assume my brother could be bought. He couldn't. His own family knew it best.

Tommie talked on the phone with Hal almost every day. He was a buyer for Saks Fifth Avenue, and went to work later and came home earlier than my father, who slaved away for Channel 13. I think he made more money than Dad did. I don't know how I knew this but I did know it, even as a little kid. It made Hal interesting to me, but it embarrassed me sometimes that my father couldn't keep up with someone who went into the city and tried on clothes all morning and ate a big, late lunch and came home. That was how I imagined the life of a buyer.

As soon as he got home he'd call us, or Tommie would call him. They sometimes spent an hour on the phone. We had a black wall phone in the kitchen and Tommie would sit at the table doing the crossword puzzle while she talked. Hal made her laugh. She never laughed much with us, and never in the same youthful way she did with him. Without knowing it she'd play with the phone cord, wrapping her finger around it, then letting it go. Sometimes she'd say, "We know what *that* means," and roll her eyes. I thought I'd give anything to be in on the secret.

When I was eleven or twelve there was another secret. Tommie would say, with what seemed like genuine impatience, "Don't be a jackass, Hal. Marry her." He finally did get married to a young woman from Iceland with red hair. That lasted about six months. Her name was Erica and she liked me to call her Mrs. Chapin. Tommie said Mrs. Chapin or not, she was young enough to be my sister, but I think she was in her late twenties. She didn't like my mother, and at the end, at one of

Hal's parties, she chased my father around a table, then kissed him on the mouth. Pack your bags, said Hal. Sleep on the couch, said Tommie. It was a card table, I later found out, and Dad had not tried his hardest to escape the seduction.

After Erica left, everything that was about to change between our two houses, changed. Hal didn't come home for days at a time. He must have stayed in the city. At dark I'd look up from my homework, out across the field to see his lights go on. They went on automatically, one upstairs and one down, to prevent robberies. A couple of years went by before he started having parties again, and they were smaller and quieter, and the couples were mostly men. No one got drunk and fell in the pool. Everyone brought a little something to eat. Around midnight, he would dim the lights on the veranda and sing "Goodnight, Ladies," then send everyone home. Sometimes Dad and Mom went. Dad said he missed the old feline energy of Hal's parties. "Meaning redheads," said Tommie. What she missed was the dancing, a hired band, catered hors d'oeuvres, booze. "I love drinking gin out of a rented glass. There's nothing like it, Helen, nothing on earth."

After "Goodnight, Ladies" Dad would come home. He'd drive the car home and later, when Tommie felt like it, she'd walk home across the field. I don't know why they even took the car, unless Dad didn't like people to know he was the neighbor. I asked him once and he said, "It's just more normal, Helen."

I was a freshman in high school and Brighton was a junior, though he should have been a senior. He had tuberculosis when he was seven and missed so much school they kept him back a grade. He was in the same sullen phase of life he'd been in since he was eight — longer than any of us thought possible. We were not getting used to it, at least I wasn't. Proof of this was that every time I saw him, which wasn't often, though we lived in the same house and went to the same school, I would attempt some sort of communication, a hello or a hiya, Brighty. I couldn't get it through my head that my brother was not available. Not to me, not to anyone. And to my knowledge, he wasn't even on drugs.

In the early spring I was over at Hal's a lot. I told him on the first warm day I'd paint the pool for him. He said I didn't need to paint the pool, I could just use it and enjoy it when the weather got good. I said I used it more than anyone else and he said that was what it was there for. He said he'd pay somebody to paint it and I said if he was going to do that he might as well pay me. He laughed and said I ought to get Dad to find me a job at Channel 13, I had the head for it. I said I wasn't interested in Channel 13, and anyway I was just in high school.

Hal paid me five dollars an hour, which was too much to pay a kid. He fed me lunch every day — curried egg salad, or cold steak sandwiches on homemade bread, and cookies and Coke — and he never stopped the clock. He hung around and talked, mostly about himself and sometimes about Tommie, or he played opera in the house with all the windows open and came out to tell me what I was listening to and how it might look on stage and who had sung it. I liked him. He was different from a lot of people. And he liked me. I wanted to be liked.

One day he asked about Brighton and I told him he was seeing a psychiatrist in New York.

"So that's what he does every Friday. He's a stone-faced kid, your brother. Sometimes we're on the same train out and I offer him a lift, but he's scared to get in a car with me."

"He doesn't like driving unless he drives. Also, he doesn't like men."

Hal let that go and asked, "Who's he seeing?"

"You mean what doctor?"

"Yeah."

"I don't know. Tommie found him."

"I bet it's David Pearlman. He's good. He's expensive. But he's a man."

"How do you know him?"

"I know a lot of shrinks."

"Why? They're all gay?"

He laughed. "I don't know them socially."

It was the first time I'd used "gay" in front of Hal and it felt daring. I experienced a lift in my chest. My heart raced and I got hot in the face. If he noticed, he didn't say anything. He'd taught me the word, after all. I knew the options. At school you called people queer or faggot or fag or pansy if you didn't like them. Hal said you could say gay or you could say homosexual. Homosexual was more formal, more medical. Gay was emotional and political. But test the waters, he advised. Listen before you open your mouth. That was what he did, and he wasn't so old at the game either.

He brought home his first love, a boy called Danny, when he was my age. He didn't think they were sweethearts, he just knew they longed for the same thing. They were two prep school boys, arriving in Hal's mother's apartment with duffel bags full of dirty socks and Ovid. It was spring break. New York smelled of soil and gave off its spring illusion of warmth right above head level. Green buds shot out and up. Wind shook the trees. For a week they went everywhere together — to museums, to movies, on long walks in the park. Danny wanted to take a subway down to Greenwich Village. He knew what he knew. But Hal said no.

One night, as they were walking downtown to see a play, the streetlights failed. The power went out as far as they could see up and down Broadway, and in the same split second they reached for each other's hand. They walked to the theater that way and sat in the theater, hands touching, sides brushing electrically in the dark. Afterwards, they went to an all-night coffee shop, then I think they went home and made love.

Hal told me these things piece by piece, as if to deny gravity by distracting it from its own laws. I was never overwhelmed by his stories. They were never shocking, always hazy and vague when it came to sexual particulars. But he did educate me, slowly, as to his life. In the two years since Erica left he'd lost forty pounds, bought some new clothes and a set of expensive French cookware. He dug a hole by the swimming pool and put in a whirlpool bath with hot and cold jets, underwater lights, a surface like the head on a glass of beer. He was learning something about himself and we all knew it. It reminded us of what we ourselves were afraid to know. We had, as a family, already begun to crack. We gave it the name Brighton, and soon enough we called it Tommie, and finally it was my turn. Only Dad was spared the cockeyed voyage. As he said, somebody had to stay behind to make the beds.

After supper every night, Brighty went out to be by himself, to walk around like a little man in the world. Dad and I sat in the kitchen reading the paper, and Tommie read or watched television in the living room. After a while, she'd miss us and come in and want to go to a movie, or on a school night go for a drive. She was trying to teach me how to drive. She thought I should become independent as soon as possible.

"That's idiotic," said Dad, who thought I was independent enough. "She can't get her license for another two and a half years. What's the point of learning now? She'll just have to learn again."

Tommie laughed. "You don't forget how to drive. It's like walking, Frank."

"I really don't want to learn, Mom."

"Oh, come on. Why not? We'll take the car to Snow Field. Your father can sit in the back and read the paper. It'll be fun."

"I just don't want to go. It'll be dark. I don't want to learn to drive in the dark."

My father looked at his watch. "Should we be worried about Brighton?"

"It won't be dark," said Tommie. "They turn the lights on. What do you think, they play baseball in the dark?"

"You mean there's a game going on?"

"Of course there's a game going on, but not in the parking lot. They have that big parking lot and I've been thinking it's the perfect place for you to learn. But if you don't want to learn —"

"I didn't say I didn't want to learn. I just don't want to learn now, at night, with all these people I know watching me."

"Who's watching you?"

"Everyone. Teachers. Certain boys. I have to go to school here, Tommie, and you don't. It makes a difference."

"I'm going out to look for him," said Dad. He put the paper down and got up and went out the side door to the garage. We heard the car start and move away down the driveway.

"He worries about him," said Tommie.

"Don't you?"

"Not in the same way. If he got in trouble I'd feel it, and I don't feel it. If you're a mother you feel these things. Your father doesn't have that to go by."

"So you can read his mind?"

"Whose?"

"Brighty's."

"No. I don't think anyone can read the mind of an adolescent boy, except someone who's been one."

"That's a lot of people, Mom. That means Dad can."

"Maybe he can. But actual danger to Brighton is something I'm better at sensing."

"I can sense it."

Just then Brighton walked in, opened the refrigerator and stared into it, tapping a restless foot on the floor. Somewhere along the way he'd gotten tall and horribly skinny, though he ate all the time. He was beautiful as a kid, blond curls to his shoulder that Tommie and Dad did battle over — my mother hiding the scissors and my father stealing him from his crib at nap time to take him to the barber. Now he was hard to look at. Thin brown hair, greasy and stringy, always in his face. A bad case of acne. Chapped lips. A habit of blinking.

"Dad's looking for you," I said.

"So?"

He took out a couple of bagels, the jar of peanut butter, a quart of milk, and headed off to his room.

"Do we ever see that milk again?" I asked Tommie.

One night after Brighty went on the prowl, I said to my parents, "If who he's seeing is David Pearlman, Hal knows him." I just thought it was interesting.

Dad put down the paper and said, "How the hell does Hal know Brighton's seeing a doctor? Will you tell me that?"

"It's obvious how he knows," said Tommie.

"Sure," I said, "I told him."

"Good God," said my father. "Is there no such thing as discretion between neighbors? I don't go poking my nose in his life, why should he go poking his nose in mine?"

"Your life?" said Tommie. "I thought we were talking about your son."

"He didn't poke his nose in, Dad. I told him."

"Where's your judgment, Helen? Put yourself in your brother's shoes."

I appealed to Tommie. "What did I do?"

"It sounds to me like you told a family secret."

"Let's not go calling it a secret. It's not a secret," said my father.

"Sure it is," she said. "That's why Hal didn't hear it from me. Brighton's one big secret these days and he has been for years, don't kid yourself. He's not coming back to us. Give up on it. Sometimes you insult your own intelligence."

"Of course he's coming back to us. He lives here. This is his home."

Tommie shook her head. "Deaf ears, Frank."

He got up and went out to look for Brighty. He did it every night now. Brighty always came back, the physical body of Brighton did, either with Dad or on his own. With Dad he sat melted up against the passenger door, looking like his best friend, the anonymity of darkness, had just died. I don't know what it took for my father to coax him in, animal to trap. I bet not much. Brighton knew the sooner done the sooner over with. External resistance wasn't his style; he just went all inside. Once when I watched them arrive, two lonely men on a raft in the ocean, pulling into the garage, I thought how happy I was not to be either of them.

Dad drove an old green Volvo sedan. It was his station car, his car for night riding, the car he took to Hal's parties and home again, with or without Tommie. It had two hundred thousand miles on it. I had grown up in it. It had brown leather seats, and ashtrays built into the leather door handles. There was a booster seat in the middle of the back seat where Brighton and I used to fight for king-of-the-castle.

For years we were a one-car family like everyone else. The morning routine meant up, dress, eat and out the door by seven. Dark in the winter. I was slow like a bear hibernating, and "Hurry up, Helen!" echoed around the house. Tommie drove. First to the station where I began to wake up as the crossing bells rang and flashed red, a full minute ahead of the train. Cars of wives and kids pulled up next to us, kids we went to school with and wives Tommie knew. The husband leaned to kiss the wife, tousle the kids, then jumped out and raced to the platform. Someone forgot his briefcase and a boy or girl flew from the car — I did it once and my heart pounded for an hour — flew towards the father and train with the briefcase held out as if weightless, the wife honking, siblings yelling, a sound and scene which happened regularly and made every man on his way to the city stop, squeeze his hand to feel the leather handle of his life's work, and calm himself, all in one motion. The one time it was my father and I came running towards him with the prize, the look on his face was of angry embarrassment, hidden by smugness, something he seemed to have willed to Brighton.

Tommie took us to school after that, and she herself went home via the market, chatted with the butcher, bought a pot roast for supper, then spent the day preparing for the next time she'd see us. She wrote lists of things to do and lost them all over the house: thaw string beans, call Dr. Sam, organize attic, shoes for B, find math book. She was always tutoring one of us in something, that time me in math. What a strange life.

"Not so strange, Helen. You forget, we all did it. It gave me a chance to get to know my kids at least." No wonder she could look at my father and say of their son, he's not coming back to us. She'd spent Brighty's whole life turning him over and over in her palm like a silken stone.

Dad was like a war father, heroic in a different country. We got the gist of him and he of us, but the real stuff was seldom laid bare. Tommie was right. He did insult his intelligence, and ours too. He still thought he could make us into something — Brighton into a good strong boy, and me a little less strong, a little more narrow-minded. But we were something already. He had missed it. He got on the train in the morning and sped away from our lives, and didn't see that as he left us, we left him. He thought because he came back to us at night, we did the same; that our journey was practical, as his was, and enjoyable in its way in the company of others just like us. Brighton showed him otherwise, and before long Tommie did too, and I did, and Hal over there in his empty house, straining against failed connection and the difficulty of knowing oneself. I will never forget those first hopeful notes of "Goodnight, Ladies," the way they rose from Hal's yearning and wobbled across the field and up into my bedroom where I waited for them with a similar yearning. I wanted the world to sleep peacefully, and I wanted not to be Helen. I wanted to be someone already changed, looking back on who she was before she became unknown to herself.

Brighton

When I was the prince of rashes, Mom put gloves on me at night so I couldn't scratch and bleed and ruin her sheets. I could just rub myself raw. They were her old gloves. She said they were the gloves she met Dad in. They were yellowed white cotton and they came halfway up my arms. Some kids say prayers. We said goodnight to the hands. I don't ever remember sleeping without them.

First we put cold cream inside for the rashes on my palms, then she taped them on me. In the morning she came in and cut the tape and woke me up and I shook the gloves off and I was a free man. A free little boy. Then as the day went on I'd start to miss them. Especially in winter when the skin peeled off my palms. Kids didn't like to touch me when they saw I was made of paper. I was the paper boy. I was the paper prince. If I could hide my hands somewhere I was free.

When I got older, like eight maybe, I'd wake up in the night and rip the tape off with my teeth, rip the gloves off, wipe the cold cream on the sheet and bite the dead skin off. Sometimes I'd keep it in my mouth until it turned soft and stuck to my tongue. Sometimes I'd swallow it.

Pearlman asks if I was self-stimulating at the time. Self-stimulating? What the fuck? Masturbating, he says. Did the prince jack off? I turn and look out the window and don't give him the satisfaction. Then I say, I'm going to have to like you a lot more before we talk about stuff like that.

Talk about when Faith died.

Shit. I was one and a half. What did I know? I don't remember it. I don't know anything about her except what I make up.

What does she look like?

Nervous. Blond hair.

Nervous?

Cynical. Worse than me.

Is she attractive?

I never thought about it. I know her insides better than her face. When I dream about her she doesn't have a face. I used to dream about her.

You don't now?

Sometimes I do. I don't dream much.

Tell me about her insides.

I told you, she's cynical. She's smart. She's fucking brilliant.

Why is she cynical?

You ever tried being brilliant and a girl? Try it sometime.

Who are her friends?

I'm her friend.

And your other sister? Helen?

What about her?

Is she her friend?

No. She never knew her.

You didn't know her either.

She's not her friend.

Is she your friend?

Helen? No. She's a kid. She tries too hard. She's just a kid. She doesn't know what to do with herself. She talks to the guy next door a lot.

The guy next door?

The neighbor.

Have you ever talked to Helen about Faith?

Why would I? No one talks about Faith.

You do. You just did.

Points for you, Pearlman, I say. He says, talk to Helen about Faith.

But I don't. Instead I come back and talk to Pearlman about why I can't talk to Helen about Faith. He listens. He says fine. He's got a baby face. I bet he's no older than Dad but he's losing his hair on top. He's got glasses, yellow skin, big hands. Tall. Not skinny. Big thighs. He wears khaki pants, drip-dry shirts, a cardigan, and those brainy Jewish shoes, Hush Puppies. He sits in a little white chair that looks like it came from somebody's kitchen. I sit in the black leather thing for patients. Clients. He calls us his clients. For a while he called me Mr. Haas. He asks if I mind if he smokes. He's one of those deep draggers. He inhales the way a woman does. He lets the ash go so long it drops on the rug.

He gives me an assignment: Talk to Helen about Faith. Pearlman, I say. He says, talk to Helen about Faith, Brighton. I know you can't. I know why you can't. So just go do it. You're a crock of shit, I say. He laughs.

I give myself my own assignment: talk to Faith about Helen. I'm proud of this. He's going to like it. But then I can't find

Faith, can't find her anywhere. I can't call her up or feel her at all. Fucking zero. That week she's gone.

I go to Helen without her. I sit on her bed. I say, can I sit here? She says, well yeah, sure. She's sitting at the window doing her homework and she thinks I'm just there to sit on her bed. Finally I say, you want to talk? She looks at me like I shit on her bed. Yeah, she says. Talk? Sure. What do you want to talk about? She's pretty, Helen. When did she get pretty? Not pretty exactly, but grown-up looking. She's got these long legs now. I never saw those legs before. She sweeps them out from under the desk and around so she's facing me. Are you okay, Brighty? What's happening? I tell her she could use a haircut. She pats her hair like she never knew it was part of her until I said that. Oh yeah, I guess I could, she says. She really tries, Helen does. I think in a few years she's going to be really pissed off.

What's school like? I say.

Oh, you know. Pretty regular.

You like anyone?

You mean teachers?

No. Like boys or something. Do you have any friends?

I've got friends.

Not boyfriends?

No. Are you kidding? She looks out the window and looks back. I think boys are pretty pathetic. Anyway, why are we talking about this?

I don't know.

I'm on some teams, she says. She's got her knee up and she's drawing on it.

Basketball, right?

Yeah.

That's it?

Well, yeah. It's a lot of work. I like the other girls on the team. I think they like me. They're older. Some girls from your class are on it. Lisa Hall. Do you know her? How about Carol Stefaniac? Or that other one. What's her name? She's from Holland. I forget her name. She's tall and really skinny and she has this white skin. She has an accent.

I don't know her.

I bet you do. If I could just think of her name. She's really nice. She's from Holland.

I don't know her, Helen. Well, I better get going. You're doing your homework?

Yeah, math.

I stink at math.

I stink at it too. Where are you going?

Just out, you know.

Oh, right. Well. Come by again if you want.

Yeah, okay, and I go.

What do I do when I go out at night? The first thing I do is tell all my thoughts to shut up. This is their time to shut up, and they do. Mostly I try and find Faith and talk to her. That's different from thinking. When I'm talking to people I'm not thinking. I tell this to Pearlman and he says, you like thinking.

Yeah, I guess. I never thought about it.

I like thinking too.

Well, yeah. What else is there?

Oh, there's lots of things. There's what you do on walks.

You mean talking to people?

There's that too.

That's what I do on my walks.

You talk to Faith. That's not people, Brighton. Faith is someone you make up. She'll never disappoint you. That's the difference between her and people.

[21]

I look out the window. I want to fight with him but it's too late. He said something he believes. I don't know if I believe it. I get up and go to the window. It's the window I've looked out all this time and I've never gone to it, never stood by it and looked down into the city where we are now, this man David and I. I think about when Dad comes after me in the car. Dad who hardly ever reads a book. I don't know if he ever thinks. I don't know who he is, I'll never know. When he comes after me at night he drives along the edge of the road like an old man. He's not even going five miles an hour. He's got his parking lights on, his headlights off. I say why do you do that? I don't want to scare you, he says. Keep the headlights on and drive like a regular person. You won't scare me. You don't need to come after me.

He must be so afraid of life. I see this out the window. I see little Faith dying on her birthday. I see him leaning across the front seat to open the car door for me. When I close it he tells me it's not closed. It's closed, Dad. No, it doesn't sound closed, slam it. Sometimes I slam it, sometimes I don't. If I don't he worries the whole way home, if I do he still worries. He says nothing. We don't know how to talk.

I say, David?

Yes?

Do you talk to your dad?

I used to.

What did you talk about?

He laughs. He looks embarrassed. He says, well, we talked mostly about God. We read the Torah together.

What happened?

What happened?

Why did you stop talking?

Oh. Well, he died.

At the end of the session I ask him, so the Torah, that's like the Old Testament, right? Right, he says. Your dad, what was he, some kind of scholar? He was a rabbi, says David. Really, a rabbi? That's cool. I guess it's cool, says David. He could be kind of a windbag.

The next time I see David is two weeks later. He's tan and he looks like he put on a little weight. He actually looks good, he looks healthy. Where did you go? I say. He says, Florida. You have a place down there? He looks embarrassed and says well, yeah, a small place, an apartment. You went by yourself? No. Who'd you go with? With friends, he says, with a friend. He looks at his watch in an obvious way and I say, okay, your hour's up, let's shrink me now. I like that I say it.

He's sort of disorganized today, and very serious. Usually I'm the serious one. Maybe feeling unprepared makes you serious. He's going through his notes in his lap and I say, so how's the habit? He looks at me and I say, the smokes? You put on a little weight so I thought maybe you quit, like, on your vacation.

It wasn't that kind of vacation, he says.

Oh. I mean, not a lot of weight. It's good. You look good.

Thanks. He takes his jacket off and gets up and goes to the window. It's almost spring out there. It's March. I bet he wishes he was still in Florida. This pigeon comes to the ledge. They're weird birds. I like them. It's weird to think that they fly. They don't even look athletic.

David says, do you have friends? He leaves the window and comes and sits down. Who are your friends? He puts his notes on the floor. I never see him write anything down but he's got all these notes. I get a little paranoid when I see notes everywhere. I ask him, are all those notes about me? He says yes. What do you write down? Oh, things I'm not likely to remember. Like what? Like what, he says. Well, let's see. He goes for the notes and I say, to me it's creepy that you have, you know, like my life there. Creepy? he says. Why creepy? Well, I mean the wrong person could get hold of it and, I don't know, use it I guess. What are you saying, Brighton? Say what you're saying. That tone of voice pisses me off and I tell him, I said what I'm fucking saying. They freak me out, okay? I feel like you're spying on me. Like I'm in front of a camera all the time. But it's a hidden camera. You get to hide behind it and I get to sit here in front of it and be fucked-up and confused, like some dumb, fucked-up kid. Like that question, who are my friends? Fuck you, who are my friends. You know the answer to that. Faith, period. And that goes down on the record. Friends, zero. Nice guy, Brighton Haas. Normal, friendly guy. Just a regular guy. No friends. You know what that is, David? It's embarrassing, that's what it is. It's fucking humiliating. I don't think it's good for me, this thing we've got going. I don't like it anymore. It's too unequal.

And you know what he says, the asshole, he says, say what you're saying, Brighton. I still don't know what you're saying. Like I pour my guts out and he's not even listening. I can't believe it. I just stare at my sweater and what do I feel? I don't even feel mad. I just feel like I give up, like it's over, something is over, like something died.

He says, you're asking me to be your friend and I can't be, that's all. I'm your advocate. I'm your intercessor. I'm your doctor. I may be your confessor, but that's up to you. What you say in here is up to you. It's totally confidential, you know that. We went over that at the beginning and you understood it then, you trusted it. Which is why I say, say what you're saying. It's not about confidentiality, it's about mutuality, isn't it? In your words: it's too unequal. Well, it has to be. You're paying me and

STEERFORTH PRESS

Post Office Box 70

South Royalton, VT 05068

STEER
FORTH
PRESS

Founded in 1993, Steerforth Press is committed to publishing serious works of prose, both fiction and non-fiction. Our interests as publishers fall into no particular category or field and our only tests of a book's worth are whether it has been written well, is intended to engage the full attention of the reader, and has something new or important to say. Steerforth's books should be available at your bookstore, and most booksellers will special order any book not in stock. If you would like to know about other Steerforth books or forthcoming titles, please return this card and we will send you our catalogs twice-yearly at no charge. You may also visit our website at *www.steerforth.com*.

Name

Street Address or Post Office Box

City State Zip

In which book did you find this card?

I'm providing a service, like the Maytag man. Friends are other kinds of people, Brighton. You don't have to be as honest with friends as you are with me. You can have fun with them. You can goof off. Do you ever goof off?

I don't know. No.

Try it this week. That's your assignment. Goof off twice this week.

I don't know what you mean. You mean just be stupid?

No. Just be a little more carefree.

I'm supposed to try and be carefree? That seems stupid.

David laughs. Just be a little more like you were at the beginning of the session. Do you remember how that felt?

Yeah. I think so.

Well, see if you can find it again.

On the train I figure out what he's saying. He's saying don't be so fucking uptight.

There's this girl, Maria, who's like a black belt in karate. Well, black, I don't know, but some kind of belt. She can flip me, no problem. To me that's a black belt. She's a senior. She's Italian, and that's how she looks. Green skin, black hair. I don't look at eyes so much, so I don't know about her eyes. They're black, I bet. Her last name is DiAngelo, of the angels. That's heavy, I tell her. I tease her about it, like it's a big responsibility.

Our school is pretty small so I'd seen her before in the hall, where you see people. She always had these big guys around her, not on her arm or anything, but like they were stuck to her character. She says no, they were hooked on her personality. I think it's great that someone like her can be inside a situation like that and still know what's really going on.

She's not a cheerleader or anything. She's not even really popular. She's pretty, I guess. Helen knows her and she says she's pretty. But she's not beautiful. And she does this weird karate stuff that a lot of people think is just about killing people and fighting and splitting boards in half with your bare hands. Maria says it's not like that, it's not about that. It teaches you to be peaceful.

The way we met is funny. I was walking by her locker and she was standing there yelling at a guy named George Washington, calling him a coward and a pervert. That's his real name, George Washington. He's a kid in my class, a total jerk. His family's really fucked-up, I think. Anyway, he's got a lot of problems. Maria's saying she knows he did it, and how disgusting it is, and what a negative way to get attention. That really surprised me, that last part. It sounded so psychological and I never thought of her that way before. I was almost past them and suddenly she says, ask this guy, and jumps in front of me so I almost run into her. She does that a lot, she uses her body to stop people. It's the karate, but now that I know her better I know it's also because she doesn't trust her voice, really. That's why she yells. It's the way she grew up. She thinks if you're yelling, maybe they'll hear you, but if you're just talking in a regular voice, that's like a whisper. It's sort of a joke with us that we met because here I am, I can hardly talk at all at school and Maria can only yell. And laugh. She can laugh. I like that about her too.

Outside of school, I talk more and she yells less. She still laughs more than I do, but people don't change in a day. Maybe they don't change, period. What do you think, Maria? This is the kind of stuff we talk about.

I think people do change. She says it depends if you mean personality or character. Character doesn't change. We agree on that. I say it's like the basement. Rock bottom. Most people

I would have to explain that to, but she gets it. I like that about her.

What George Washington had done was put a naked picture of himself on the wall in the girl's bathroom. What made him a coward was that he chopped the head off. How did you know it was George? I asked her. She said if you observed people, which you don't Brighton, you didn't need to see them dressed to know who they were.

She was the first person outside of my family who knew I was going to a shrink. I think. Sometimes I think Hal Chapin knows, just by the way he says hi to me on the train but he never tries to sit next to me. Most people, if they sort of know you and you're on an empty train together and they don't see you every day, they'll sit next to you. They feel like they have to. You both feel trapped. But if they know you've just been to the shrink and you're, like, a little kooky, they're not going to bother. They're going to give you that little wave like Hal does, and if they've got kids they're going to keep their kids behind them and count heads and push them down the aisle to another seat. Then they're going to whisper things you can hear all the way down at the other end of the train. Mom did that with us on a train where there was a crazy lady who was an old friend of hers. She was either crazy or drunk.

When he gives me a lift from the station he doesn't say much either. It's like a ten-minute drive. Well, five-minute. It takes an hour to walk. With Mom he's pretty talkative, and with Helen he talks his head off. But for the whole time we're in the car together he doesn't ask me anything or even really say stuff about his work or, you know, the weather or anything. He just drives.

I think maybe he hates me. I tell this to Pearlman and he says, because he doesn't talk much, he hates you?

Well, yeah. And he doesn't sit next to me on the train.

Do you want him to?

No. I hate that shit, when people do stuff to be polite.

So he leaves you alone, and that's why he hates you?

Yeah. Well, I mean, no. It's just that I know when he's around Mom or Helen he talks a lot.

How about with your father?

They don't talk. Dad doesn't talk to anyone.

So he talks to the women and not to the men?

Yeah. I guess.

Who do you talk to, Brighton?

Um, well, Maria. Mom sometimes. A little to Helen.

You used to talk to Faith, says David.

I still do.

Maria, Mom, Helen, Faith. That's an all-girl team, isn't it?

Well, yeah.

Do you see what I'm getting at?

Not really.

Men often have an easier time talking to women than to other men. If he doesn't talk to you, it might not mean that he hates you. Why does he hate you, Brighton?

It's just a gut feeling.

Where does the feeling come from?

My gut.

He laughs. What gives you the feeling?

I don't know. Stuff he says.

I thought he didn't talk.

I said he didn't talk much. Sometimes he says stuff. Like last Friday he asked me if I liked the theater. I said, you mean plays and shit? He said, yeah, plays and shit. Well, that to me sounded like he was making fun of me. It pissed me off. I told him, oh yeah, the theater. Nah, I don't like it, it's too faggy.

End of story? says David.

No. He said opera was faggier.

That's quite a conversation. Who do you think was more pissed off, you or him?

I was. I don't think he was pissed off. He didn't act like it.

Don't you hate that, says David.

What?

When people are better actors than you are?

Maria gave me this book on Buddhism, which sounds dull but it's really pretty interesting. They burn a lot of incense in that religion and the book explains why. It's because the Buddhas think the human body smells really terrible. When I read that I thought, wow, I could be a Buddhist, no problem. I said this to Mom. I explained to her about the book and this thing about how humans stink, which is pretty funny, right? but also true. Like, really true. I said, that kind of religion makes sense to me. Where there's something you do and a reason for it. It's not all that abstract shit. She said, what's so abstract about being an Episcopalian? You've got this rock solid Trinity. It all hangs on that. This Father, Son, Holy Ghost thing that we're all supposed to swallow whole and spit back out again to our kids. Brighton, believe me. Any religion you want to take on, take it on, boy-o, with my blessing. But why trade one unimaginative faith for another? You know what I mean?

She's strange these days, Mom is. That boy-o. I go in to Helen and ask if she thinks Mom's acting strange.

She's getting drunk a lot, says Helen.

You're kidding. How do you know that? I just talked to her and she wasn't drunk. I don't think she was.

At night, I mean.

Not every night.

You don't see it, Brighty. You go out. Then Dad goes out after you. I see it.

What? Like a beer?

No, not like a beer.

Well, what?

Forget it. She turns her back and drums her pencil on her desk.

Don't be a pain, Helen.

Don't you be a pain. She doesn't like beer. She hates beer. Have you ever seen her drink a beer? She never drinks beer. She drinks gin. She puts it in milk. It's gross.

In milk? No way.

In hot milk.

No way.

Oh, shut up, she says. Just shut up. She puts her head down on her desk and points to the door. I go.

Tommie

I was born Margaret Fair Thomas, back when the world began, and called Margot, which I hated. I went away to college where everyone was called Margot, or Maggie, or Margy, or Margie, or Meg, or Peg, or Peggy, or Marge, and became Tommie. I liked it very much, thank you. My roommate, a chunky girl with heavenly skin called Jeanne Ann Love, also liked it. She sat on my bed one day, picking a cuticle. She looked up and said, "Wasn't that Eleanor Roosevelt's lover?"

"Tommie?"

"Right."

"A woman?"

"Right. Her lover or her secretary."

"I didn't know she — "

"Don't worry. It suits you, Margot."

Frank Haas was the first man I introduced myself to as Tommie, the first man who wasn't Hal. We were matched up by height at a college mixer, and what I liked about him was that he wasn't a basketball player. Tall girls always get stuck with the basketball team, most of them dopey and drooly boys with big hands like puppies. Frank was to puppy what I was to Miss America. He said, "Hi, I'm Frank. My interests are history and biology. What about you?"

"I'm Tommie," I said. "I'm interested in getting married and having a family." I didn't say, I'm interested in going to bed with you, because I wasn't. I was perfectly happy with Jeanne Ann.

Frank can't tolerate a lack of ambiguity. Mine made him quake, and he gave me up after only one dance. I wasn't disappointed. He was, and still is, not a brilliant dancer. The holding close is confusing to him and he can't let go of his own feet. How a man dances is how he'll raise his kids — Tommie's Maxim Number One. Frank is that, just that kind of father.

So I spent the evening, as I spent most evenings, in the company of Hal and Jeanne Ann, both of whom had also been dumped by their dates. Jeanne Ann was too mannish for most boys, and too boyish for most men. She wore her hair short, not hiding the breadth of her shoulders (she was a swimmer), nor the slight, not unattractive (to me), thickness of her neck. Because she was athletic, unlike me who stirred cream into tea for exercise, whatever gowny thing she put on her body ended up looking like a costume, somebody else's too tight-fitting costume, squashing her breasts and pinching her underarms and generally desecrating publicly those parts of her flesh I worshipped privately. We didn't go to many of these dances, thank God. And Hal, our mascot, our friend, was never fully appreciated by a young deb. As soon as her eye started roving he'd dance her to the edge, introduce her to some handsome frat boy and run. Poor girlie. Caught up in her post-war dream of diapers, as we all were. Maxim Number Two: On the right night, with the right man, even shit smells sweet.

My attraction to people is an attraction to their possibilities. I meet someone, and it's rare I don't picture them naked and having sex with me. I ask myself, would I like to be their lover? This happens to all of us, I know it does. It's just that people are such liars — Maxim Number Three. Having bedded them mentally, I ask myself (all this in a second or two, I'm not talking about reverie, it's quite matter-of-fact), will this person be present at my death? I call these the Two Questions. Not riddles. If the Two Questions don't appear in the first few minutes of the first encounter, they never will. It can't be helped. The click isn't there. It's a sex click, it's the click of eros and inspiration, of knowing and being known. I can name only one person who came into my life *sans clic* and has remained in it over time. It was there when I met Jeanne Ann, and a few weeks later when I met Hal. Big bingo. Anyone I talk about as my friend or lover. Anyone but Frank.

Never mind. He had qualities. He was my height. We were married. People marry for a thousand reasons, and only one of them is love. And only one of them is great sex. And only one of them is because at the end, at the deathbed, they will be there. What wife is outlived by her husband, anyway? Precious few.

I was pregnant with Helen, well into my pregnancy, when Jeanne Ann came to visit. The first time since little Faith's burial. She had been, for a day, that child's godmother. I was excited as hell to see her. Frank was less so. For one thing, whenever she came, she and I sat inside for hours at a stretch, watching doubleheaders. It was the one thing I could comfortably do with a bowling ball on my belly, and it was faintly athletic. I was supposed to be walking to bring the baby down, to get her moving. Why not baseball? I knew I had a little girl inside me. Don't ask me how I knew, I just knew. Faith's little emissary, her thank you card.

Frank doesn't like baseball. He doesn't understand it. He understands it the way he understands women, as complicated geometry around which men maneuver in order to gain points and win. So he moped in the kitchen while the two gals hooted in the living room. We had a great time. We drank wine in the middle of the day. A week went by. Who was taking care of Brighton? We were, I suppose. Jeanne Ann was. He was a very shy and serious three-year-old, just her kind of man. And then in the middle of the fun, Frank ruined it. He said go home. He gave her the boot. I didn't stand up to him for once. I blame it on the pregnancy. Though it should have been me banished from the house. It should have been both of us.

Jeanne Ann was a little bit drunk one night, which in itself riled my abstemious husband, and she said something about wasn't it funny that people got married. That was Frank's cue. He said it didn't seem funny to him, it seemed very natural, and Jeanne Ann said what she meant was, wasn't it funny the three of us (I remember thinking four, baby inside me) were rewriting history in a way.

"You lost me on that one," he said.

"We're all lost," said Jeanne Ann, and laughed in her marvelous, mouth-open way. "I named your wife, Frank. That's a piece of history I bet you never knew." It wasn't true. I named myself and Jeanne Ann was there. "I named her after Eleanor Roosevelt's lover. Don't give me that look. Yes, a woman. But in our little version, Tommie gets Franklin and Jeanne Ann gets who knows who."

That was as far as it went. I thought it was innocent enough. I thought *I* was innocent enough. That was what mattered. We all went to bed. It was a tiny, two-bedroom house, and Jeanne Ann slept downstairs with Brighton, on one of his twin beds. Frank went up to our room and I stayed behind as I had every night of our visit to kiss her goodnight — or good-bye. It felt like both. They were not profound kisses. We didn't struggle and tear at each other's clothing, though we did for the moment of the kiss instinctively retreat to her bedroom where I always checked my son's sleep before our lips met. I was a mother, so new to it, so newly reasonable since the death of Faith, I didn't believe it was possible to be two things at once, mother and lover both. This stood between me and Frank. It troubled us. It muddied our marriage. And I assumed, had assumed until that night, that what held true for husband and wife, held true for the world. They had not been lovers' kisses, mine and Jeanne Ann's. They had been heart and innocence.

This night I checked Brighton's breathing and found, as always, the steady rhythm of sleep. "Why do you do that?" she whispered. We stood behind the half-closed door and she embraced me over the hump of my belly. "He's three years old. He won't go away. If they get this far, Tommie, they're here. Don't you know that?"

She was shorter than I. She reached up and pushed the hair from my forehead. Until that moment I'd thought what concerned me was Brighton's awakeness, not his aliveness. But she was right. It was a ritual to ward off death, this checking, and the boil in my stomach wasn't the anticipation of what had been, after all, a series of sedate bedtime kisses. It was fear for my little son, for his life. Thank you, Jeanne Ann. Knowledge unleashes hormones — Tommie's Maxim Number Four. We kissed in the doorway for a long time, not by moonlight, nor starlight, but in the yellow wash of Brighty's Donald Duck night light. Only when he turned over in his sleep did we stop.

Frank came down for a glass of milk, just like a little boy, and I went upstairs with him to be a married woman again. In a lucid moment in bed I wondered what he knew, this man beside me. He was awake too, which meant he knew something. He's the kind of man who can sleep eight hours, dead to the world as they say. His head hits the pillow and he's gone. A third of the day is accounted for. And he says he doesn't even dream. I don't envy him that, though the easy sleep anyone would be jealous of. I waited to see if one of us would start talking. Neither of us did. It was a restless bed.

In the morning after an awkward breakfast, he had me drive him to the station so we could have a few minutes alone. He kissed me in the car, just to make sure all the old feelings were intact. He must have decided they were or they weren't, because he kissed me again with unusual passion. Sometimes I forget men don't know how to talk. The kiss went on and on. I remember the thought crossed my mind to be embarrassed in front of his commuting pals who pulled up on either side of us with their erect wives driving. I never liked Frank's kisses. That's the truth and I won't keep it from you. I liked him inside me though. I like penetration. The penis is a useful tool, and just remote enough, physically distant from my face enough to allow me to let go and dream. I try not to put someone else in his place when we're making love. That seems desperate, sad and cheap. We still manage to make love once a week. That might surprise you. I do love him in those moments, a few moments a week. His vulnerability is astonishing. Any man's is. What I want is for him to come to me in that openness more often. I don't even ask for it all the time. I don't even ask for a sensual, sexy lover. Though God, I miss having sex with someone, good old unreasonable sex. Lovemaking is such a sedate and acceptable pastime for a married couple. But sex.

I have a few opinions on why women make better lovers, but I'll hold off on them. No I won't. We're all adults here. I'll tell you right now. The fine hairs are more sensitive, making the entire skin more sensitive to touch. The body that's trained genetically to wake when a baby cries, not just any baby, but that body's baby, will be more alert to subtlety of all kinds. Like when to change the rhythm of a fuck. Or when not to. The slightest restlessness of her lover, the first intrusion of a dumb thought, the smallest shift away from wild mind and she knows. She lets you get away with nothing except the whole possession of your own pleasure. Bodies are so ludicrous. A tongue can hold you captive. Two fingers in the right place at the right time can knock your socks off. Saliva can be the slippery road you ride to heaven. Maybe someday I'll have sex again—that sex. Sex where only my children have been, before they fell out of me, slippery fish, and breathed air.

Frank caught his train and I stopped by the butcher for a flank steak, then went home. It was a sweltering July day. Brighton was running naked around the house, ahead of Jeanne Ann who was chasing him with a towel. "Mommy!" he shrieked. "I have prickly heat!" Jeanne Ann had just given him a baking soda bath. Such a serious boy, and he was clearly in love with her. I let them be. I always welcomed a break from every child I had, even Faith, the memory of Faith. They take over your life, even if you're careful, and I liked my life, thank you. I wanted to hold onto it as long as I could. It was nice to have another woman in the house, someone with instincts, unruffled by chaos, explosions of milk all over the floor, glue on the furniture, sudden tears. I won't say Jeanne Ann was good with kids, not because she wasn't, she and Brighton got along famously. But as she pointed out, he was just one kid. That he happened to be mine was points in his favor. "I don't love kids," she said, "I love some kids. People get so damn sentimental about children."

"And women," I said, thinking back to Frank's kiss.

"Not all women. Mothers. Mothers and wives."

"Not all wives. Good wives."

"Are you, Tommie?" I was washing a glass and she came and stood next to me. My son was bathed and fed, put down for a nap. I was wearing a sundress and I must have looked about fifteen years old.

"No. I'm a rotten one."

She started to stroke my neck, something that made me melt and she knew it. "Good," she said.

"Is he asleep?"

"Do we have time?"

"If he's asleep we have a few hours. Once he goes out, he's out."

"We can just lie down if you want."

"I don't want. I want everything."

She smiled. "I'll go check him."

She went and immediately I missed her. I went into the bathroom to pee. Little Helen sat right on my bladder. And there was Brighty's old bath, cold and salty looking from the baking soda. I emptied the tub and ran a clean one, tepid and clear, a cool, clear bath in that hot hot house. I undressed. Jeanne Ann came in behind me and sat next to me on the edge of the tub.

"Is this for us?"

"I thought so. Wouldn't it feel good?"

"You're very pregnant, Mrs. Haas."

"Do you like it?"

"I like it very much. I like touching it."

"Frank hates it."

"Of course he does. He can't sprawl on you."

It was an awful thought, actually. Frank sprawling.

"How's my son?"

"He sends you a message."

"What's his message?"

"He says to enjoy every minute, and he'll see you when you get back."

"Does he?"

"Does he what?"

"Say that?"

We were already drifting into the dreamy talk of lovers, the lazy dreamy place of no words. I let my hand trail in the bathtub like a woman in a punt. Jeanne Ann stood up and undressed and sat down again. I didn't dare look at her whole body. I looked at her thigh, one sunburned thigh, slick with sweat and the flesh quivering. I put my hand on it to stop it and she caught my wrist and brought my hand up and placed it on her breast. Then on her cheek. Then in her mouth, my four fingers.

I don't know when we breathed as lovers. I think we held our breath for minutes at a time and didn't know it. Didn't need it. Exalted fish. She slid into the bath. I turned on the edge of the tub and sat with my feet in the water, my belly reaching out to her. She stroked it with both hands. It was bluish, the navel extended. She put her tongue on my navel, and Helen, in a sudden burst of energy borrowed from me, started kicking like the little prisoner she was. Jeanne Ann laughed. She pressed her forehead against the bulge and waited for the next blow. I had never looked at intimacy from this angle.

I can tell you everything we did that day. I can promise you I had not one thought about my husband. Helen, yes. Brighton, yes. But mostly no, none of it. We hadn't intended to end up in the bathroom. I hadn't. Bathrooms are where we go before sex.

Our changing rooms. The room of hiatus. Where the world falls away. Where we face the mirror and rinse our hands of dishes and sons. Where we ready ourselves. Where we breathe. I saw us in my bed, Jeanne Ann and me. Our bed. Mine and Frank's. I imagined us there, the two of us, fucking in my un-made bed, making a mess of my tidy marriage in no other way but the physical. A bath first, then the body. No reason to lock the bathroom door. Brighton would sleep for hours in heat like this, amazing child. And he did. But Frank came home. In the middle of the afternoon. Why? I can't tell you. He felt sick is what he said, and he looked it, he looked green. But I've never known him, before or since, to give a second thought to illness. He swats it away like a fly and goes back to work and comes home at the time he's expected. He must have caught a taxi from the station. He came into the house calling my name as I was saying Jeanne Ann's. It was a shock to me. I respond badly to surprises. The bathroom was off the kitchen, a few steps from the kitchen door, and he came in there I suppose to soak his head. He'd loosened his tie, which he rarely did — it was either on or off. It looked like a noose around his neck.

I said, "Frank."

"Oh. Tommie." He looked annoyed, like I'd just woken him from a comfortable nap. I had. "Oh," he said again. "My God."

I thought he'd go away. I wished he would. If only to give us time to organize ourselves. But he didn't. And right or wrong, I use that stubbornness of his to justify my own behavior. It wasn't necessary to do what I did next, but he made it so.

Jeanne Ann was positioned between my legs in the tub, her back up against my belly. Her eyes were closed, her head lolled backwards against my shoulder. I'd burrowed under her thigh and was inside her, had been for some time. I knew the cushiony warmth of that place. I loved it. I didn't want to leave it.

He must have been approaching the house when I whispered, "Hi."

She opened her eyes. "Hi."

"I think I'll just stay in here forever, inside here."

She closed her eyes again. "Let's go up."

"Upstairs?"

"Let's go sprawl."

I pushed deeper into her and her face tightened in concentration. "We'll go soon," I said.

A moment later I heard Frank call my name. I pulled out of her and watched in shocked amazement as the door opened and in he came, for one sweet second unknowing. Absurd how knowledge changes a life when other things don't. We might have been two friends on a sled. He was the dangerous hill. I felt Jeanne Ann about to lift herself up, God knows why. Towards the towel, possibly. Or to ward him off, to protect a pregnant woman. Just instincts. Mine were working differently. Mine were for retaliation. I was frightened. So was she. So was the dangerous hill. I pressed my thighs against hers and took the soap and slid my arms around her waist to keep her there. I felt her come back to me, just the slightest give of her shoulders. I made her come back to me, to shield me. She was the sacrifice I held up to my husband as I began to soap her belly, then each soft breast. In front of him as he watched. It was unforgivable.

Frank

If you have ever stepped onto the river at dawn, taken up your oar, drawn your chest to your knees and felt the swell of the blade pulling you and eight others through the foggy morning, you know that all meaning can reside, briefly, in the physical; pleasure is not anonymous; the ache of the body brings something to the heart. I lived in a husk, a paper boat thin as a locust skin, half my college life. I gripped a sapling and forced it through the water with six men at my back and two before me. One of the two was a light fellow named Bumpy Marvin who went on to become a first class coxswain. The other was our stroke, Ted Faneuil.

Ted was as tall as I but more powerful by half. He had straight fair hair which touched the top of his ears — a real longhair by the standards of those days. His neck and shoulders supported a head too small for the body he'd built for himself, so although he was plenty handsome he appeared at the same time comical. At least from behind, which is the angle I was best acquainted with. He had a birthmark at the base of his neck he'd never seen, I realized. I knew it so well I saw it before me sometimes instead of his face on the infrequent occasions we spoke to one another on dry land.

It would be an exaggeration to say I lived for my time in the boat. I had met the girl who would be my wife and she occupied my thoughts and some weekends. I took my studies seriously too. But nothing touched the excitement I felt those black mornings of fall, or the gray ones of spring, getting up and throwing on a T-shirt and sweatpants, socks and sneakers, all stinking of the week's exertion. No breakfast, and a run to the boathouse three miles away. Then the sky beginning to say a word or two as we carried out the boats on our shoulders, then the oars. Ted Faneuil lived the farthest away of any of us — he lived with his parents in what I learned was a raw neighborhood of New Haven — and yet he was there every morning ahead of the rest, looking laundered, slept and fed. He didn't have a car either. His mother dropped him off on her way to her job at the A & P.

I didn't think in the boat. It was the only place I didn't think. I thought right up until I lowered myself into my seat, and then my mind stopped and sensations took over. Rowing was never an easy job for me. I wasn't strong the way Ted and others were strong. I didn't work out as much as they did, though I did what was required of me. I wasn't interested in bulking up for the sake of making my life at the oars less painful. The pain was all right. The pain was pleasurable. It was real and hard and gave its own satisfaction. For every stroke Ted made, I made two: one with my body and one with my will. My will dug in at the front of the stroke where chest and knees are wed, where the power is latent in the legs, and my body joined me again on the easy glide forward. I admired men like Ted whose strength complemented their natural ability. If you watched carefully you saw he rose out of his seat on every stroke, not enough to change the balance but enough to give the whole boat an airborne quality. Ted set the tone. I believe he and Bumpy Marvin had worked something out, something to do with timing but not just that, and it made our boat far more successful than the sum of its parts.

About a month into our third season together, I realized I had dreamt several nights in a row about Ted's back. I was bothered by this, and for the first time felt uncomfortable in the boat. As much as I tried not to take it in, there was his broad back in front of me, only barely clad in an undershirt wet with sweat. I decided to speak to Ted, not about my dreams but about things that were important to me. I wanted to know what was important to him. I thought he would then become human to me, with any luck a whole person.

I had pegged him as a somewhat tongue-tied fellow whose physical gifts outshone his intelligence. Perhaps I was misled by the size of his head. I don't remember how our first conversation took place, nor precisely what we talked about, but the unveiling of Ted Faneuil began with the mention of the poet Rilke and did not end until after midnight in my room with the wake-up call for practice only five hours away. I could not sleep at all that night. I had gained a friend. He slept on the sofa in the common room down the hall, wrapped in one of my blankets.

My anatomical dreams came to an end. A few nights a week Ted and I talked. Not all of it was heady, serious stuff, though we liked that plenty and always came back to it. Sometimes he talked about being a townie and not fitting in, or being an abstemious athlete in a fraternity of budding young alcoholics whose great pleasure was to drink cheap vodka out of a boot. Midnight came and went, but in the morning he always looked rested, and his performance in the boat remained steady and strong. If anything, it improved. I didn't do well without my sleep, but the life of ideas that came to me by way of my friend was fully satisfying.

We rowed and talked our way through that season and into the next, which was our last. Tommie and I made plans to marry. One night I told Ted of these plans and after a long silence which surprised me, he surprised me even further by saying, "One thing I never told you about me, because I guess I was assuming you knew, and maybe you do know, is I'm not like you in that way. I'm not going to marry someone. I'm sorry. I'm just not." He didn't say any more and I didn't ask. We graduated soon after that and the last I heard about him was not from him but from Bumpy Marvin a year later, who wrote a letter to everyone who had ever taken up an oar with Ted, to everyone who had ever walked on water with him which is how he made us feel. *Dear teammates,* it read, *I wish I did not have to bring you the sad news of Ted Faneuil's death. Ted died suddenly at home in the house he shared with his parents. The cause of death has not been made public.* Not even *his* death, but an impersonal misfortune named death. Later I learned it was sleeping pills washed down with enough vodka to make his fraternity brothers proud.

There was more to the letter but I didn't read it. I didn't want to read a eulogy. Marvin knew Ted only from the front, a perspective I didn't have much faith in. They sat and faced each other every day, which is only the beginning of knowing someone, especially someone like Ted. I had his back. I had the part of himself he could never know or see, unless he saw it through me, which is what he spent his time doing there in my room. I thought he was happy with what he saw. Now I understood I had been wrong. One of the worst feelings in my life was to know too late that the Ted Faneuil Bumpy Marvin described was well-equipped to live, and the Ted Faneuil I knew was not.

My wife has a friend, and the friend reminds me in some ways of Ted, and my wife reminds me of me. A wilder me. A me who is wise ahead of time to what is being asked of her by her friend, though her friend may not know herself what she is asking. I don't think Ted knew what he was asking. Only after his death did I understand why we chased philosophy up and down the walls and into every corner of my room before saying good-night. My wife and her friend are not innocents like we were, and I think now it is best not to be.

Ted lived and died in the house where he was born, yet belonged nowhere. He belonged in a state of motion, out on the river, tearing a hole in the river with every stroke he took. Someone ought to have given him a boat to row for the rest of his life. My wife is that way, though she has no boat and no river. She is not at home anywhere and is therefore always moving towards something else. I live beside her as best I can. When she tires of me she goes where I cannot. When she tires of that place she comes back, and there we rest before she needs to jump her fences again. She does remind me of an unbroken horse, a horse not mine to break — not anyone's. But this is what she searches for when she goes. Someone or something to which she might submit.

Hal

Tommie spotted her first. Erica was stepping out of my pool in the only topless bathing suit I'd ever actually seen on a woman (this from the man from Saks), and Tommie, who was facing the pool, physically turned my head to catch the sight. It was late in the party and she catcalled. I said, "Don't be vulgar, darling."

"I can't help it."

"She's not at all my type. Don't even think about it."

"I'm not thinking about it. Just observing."

"You've got a better body."

"No. I've gone old around the thighs."

"I haven't seen your thighs."

"You have."

"Not recently. Not tonight. Where's Frank?"

She made a little girl pout. "All gone home."

"Well, show me. Show the doctor."

"Doctor, doctor, doctor," she said, and slipped her dress off over her head and flung it into the pool.

I know women's clothing, and I do know Tommie. That year the fashion was mini-everything, clothes made to melt like butter off bodies at just such moments as these. But Tommie wasn't fashion. She was fashion's antithesis. If you knew her you accepted that she'd arrive in an old burlap sack until that became fashionable, and then she'd find something one step more repulsive to wear. Do you see why I loved her? That night's outfit looked like a loose-fitting brillo pad. In that midsummer heat, hard to imagine. Once it became separated from her body, people felt free to make fun of it. It floated on the pool. They pounced on it. They dragged it under. It died.

We joined in the fun, if fun it was. Then we sat together, slightly sobered and dripping on the edge of the pool. I was completely dressed, a seersucker suit, white bucks. She had on what she called her native costume—a white bra and white cotton underpants that drooped around her waist. "Helen wanted to know if I wore boxers," I said.

"Of course you do."

"That's what I told her. I told her you could tell what kind of underwear a man wore by looking at his face."

"She likes you, Hal."

"I like her."

"She's going to be good looking."

"It won't faze her."

"No. Why should it? Ask that girl for a date."

"What girl?"

"The bathing suit. Miss Topless."

"Maybe," I said.

In a minute she asked me if I would do her a favor.

"It depends what it is."

"Hold my thigh."

"Hold your thigh how?"

She draped her leg across my lap and we sat there, no erection on my part — there never was with Tommie. I stroked her leg and wondered what she really needed, besides this. I knew the answer of course. It was the opposite of Frank.

I called Miss Topless that week. I called her from work, to make it a local call. How I found out who she was and where she lived was simple. Tommie told me. On her way home in my bathrobe she went up to Erica and asked her for the facts. The breasts were covered at that point. She had on a little terry cloth outfit, roughly the color of the pool. Miss Chlorine Blue.

On the phone I said I was the guy who had the party last weekend. Guy, that sounded tough enough. Tommie warned me she had an accent, she wasn't from here. What that meant to me was not New Jersey. I'd noticed she had red hair, Irish, and I was all set for Boston's unintelligible speech, those hobbled *ar*s. But it was nothing like that. On the phone I finally said, "So where are you from?"

"Iceland."

"Iceland! Christ."

"You know Reykjavik? From there."

For a month we went to movies, period. A way to beat the heat in New York. Then I'd send her off home in a cab and ease myself onto a subway to Grand Central. From there to Hoboken, and the Erie Lackawanna home. Not so much as a kiss. I liked her mind tremendously. That was how it went for me with women. If I waited, the body usually got in there too, though sometimes it didn't and I'd drag on guiltily until the other had had her fill of chastity and called it quits. Out-of-bed relationships weren't what most women were after, at least not with men, at least not with me. I had only one lasting success in that department, and that's rare enough. I think it was because we didn't have sex, Tommie and I, or if we had it (once), it only confirmed the fact that we weren't sex to each other. I think that because of this we could exercise our full range of emotions around each other. We could give, unjudged. We didn't choose husbands, wives, lovers who would allow this. Why? We had each other to fall back on and embrace. We had each other to hide in when thrown to the lions. Weren't we lucky?

Why did Tommie want me married? I think because she knew from her own marriage how little it would mean to me, and she wanted to keep our life experiences side by side. In step with each other. This is not a cynic's view. I had been dull and gloomy, depressed for several years, really since college, really since she married Frank, and she wanted to push me out into a larger life. Kids, for example. Daily relations with spouse. A sense of responsibility to that thing outside myself called the world.

What Erica and I did best was sit in smoky theaters, eyes glued to the screen, watching one foreign film after another and holding hands (sometimes). I'd lost my teenage shyness of Greenwich Village and regularly dragged us down to the Bleecker Street Theater. *La Strada, La Dolce Vita, 8½, Juliette of the Spirits.* It was a Fellini summer. Standing in line I could size up men, and the comings and goings at the Bitter End across the street. Men. I knew they meant nothing to me. Wasn't I on (or near) the arm of a young woman I would (or might) marry someday? I even involved Erica in my game, which made it all the more legitimate. I didn't have the verb "to cruise" then, but that's what it was, those lazy evenings in the Village, waiting for a film to begin. We stood in line and cruised men, my girlfriend and I. I assume she enjoyed it. She seemed to enjoy it. But I should tell you, I never really knew where her sexuality lay. I don't know Icelandic culture. We were married six months and you can share mighty little in that time. She needed to conquer with sex, but whether women would do as well as men, I have no idea. I only saw her with men. She drew them in and stunned them, then let them go. As far as I know, I was the only exception. I was not a candidate for extinction. I was only, and for a short time, her husband.

Helen the philosopher once asked me, "Why do people only marry who they don't love?" Leave out the only, I said, and move the don't to where the do is and say it again.

"Why don't people marry who they love? Why did you get married, Hal, when you didn't even like her?"

"I liked Erica."

"You didn't act like it."

"What do you mean? You can't like everybody every minute of the day."

"I know, but you never looked at each other."

"That's because we were trained at the movies."

"Whatever that means."

Helen went home, but her question hung in the air, almost visible. Why did you get married, Hal? Well, Tommie pushed it. Everyone pushed it. My mother. My dead dad. My bachelor brother Thomas, the actor. My sister Louise, with her own marriage mid-failure, and three kids. Why did you get married, Hal? To prove I wasn't gay, of course. To step away from the heat of that suggestion. Iceland is a cool and sunny place, I've heard. Even the sunshine is cool, and the water is cold and full of salmon and there's snow somewhere always. Erica became that for me, that cool refuge, if just in my mind. For in fact, the flame of her hair told me much more about who she was than where she was born ever did. Miss Topless, anything but glacial.

Too bad I married the metaphor, not the woman. What a disservice to another human life.

I take care of my mother part-time. On weekends she sends the nurses away and I move into the small room next to hers. The room has a bureau, which I don't use. I bring my things in an overnight bag and I live out of that. In the winter I hang my coat in the closet. The bed is narrow and treacherously soft. Normally I like hard beds and I like them wide enough for possibility.

Her name is Jane. I arrive on Friday evening in time to bathe her. She likes a bath before bed; it helps her sleep. I powder her. I put her diaper on. If she wants a snack I bring it to her. Whipped cream cheese on melba toast is what she likes. We say goodnight and I go into the kitchen and start making her food for tomorrow. She lives on a quiet road in Connecticut, and sometimes I just listen to the quiet, cooking and coming down off the city, or I listen to *Falstaff* on the stereo.

She often wakes in the night, but her night starts well before mine and by the time I fall asleep she's usually done with her nightmares. If they're nightmares. I don't sleep well in her house. I'm her fifty-year-old child, the age of my father when he died. Sometimes I get up and sit outside, or walk the short length of the driveway. I'm always restless. In the morning I get her up and put her on the toilet. I bathe her again. Sometimes I change her sheets. I bring her breakfast. I bring her the bedpan. Time disappears in these tasks. While she naps I listen to music or I read.

We don't talk. She can't talk. She communicates by moving her head or crying. She can point to things with her left arm. I offer to read to her but she'd rather watch television. She sleeps most of the day: getting ready for death, I guess. The way I get ready is to carry a metal bedpan with her pee and shit and dump it down the toilet. Then I go make her food.

Jane always thought Tommie was the girl I'd marry. She was the only one I ever brought home to meet her. We went to New York several times and stayed in the apartment. Tommie had my bed, I slept on the living room floor. Sometimes in the night she'd come in and lie down next to me under the blankets and we'd talk.

"Who's that a picture of in your bathroom?"

"Which one?"

"Handsome. Glasses. It looks like he's making a speech in a restaurant. He looks Mafia."

"That's Dad."

"Your dad?"

"Running for governor of Florida."

"She keeps a picture of her ex around?"

"I keep it around. It's my bathroom."

"When was he governor of Florida? Doesn't he live in Arizona?"

"And before that Texas. He's a man on the move."

"On the run?"

"Maybe. He always has been. He never made governor. You can't keep crossing state lines and make governor. He's a professional failure. That's really what he does best."

"Failure's not genetic, Hal."

"Well."

"He looks charming."

"He is charming."

"I thought he'd be blond."

"No, he's dark. Mom used to be blond. Louise and Thomas are both dark. Louise looks just like him."

"Is he married to someone?"

"Minnie."

Tommie laughed. "Minnie? Is she a mouse?"

"She is a mouse. She has black hair and green eyes, and a hundred years ago she was first runner-up for Miss Arizona."

"She wasn't."

"She was. She'll tell you all about it when you meet her."

"Will I meet her?"

"Sure. You'll meet everyone. Dad, Minnie and the whole mouse family. She has two kids, daughters, sixteen and fourteen, something like that."

"I bet they faint when you come in the room."

"I don't come in the room very often, but they don't faint. Are they old enough to faint? They must not be. They chew a lot of gum. They're addicted to gum."

"The age of gum coincides with the age of fainting."

"You know so much. Where did we ever get you?"

We lay in the dark against each other. Tommie said, "I like it here. I like your mother's taste. I think she likes me, Hal. Do you?"

"I know she likes you."

"Too bad it's for the wrong reason. It's such a boring reason."

"I love the way you say boring. Say it again."

"Boring."

"Say it again."

"I'm not saying it again. What do you think she'd say if she caught me in your bed?"

"You're supposed to be in my bed."

"I mean here on the floor with you, under the blankets."

"I think she'd say what she always says when she wakes me up in the morning."

"Which is?"

"'Breakfast, Hal. Your favorite. And bring the girl, too.' You know, she's not all that stuffy. She had a lover for a few years."

"A lover? Did he live with you?"

"Who says it was a he?"

"No, Hal. Really? A woman? A woman lover? Jane? I can't believe it."

"Too bad it's not true."

"There was no lover?"

"There was a lover. His name was Martin. Martin O'Something. I was pretty young and we didn't really see him. The sex was at his apartment, not ours."

Tommie rolled onto her side and started playing with my chest hairs. All three of them. "How can she stand it, do you think?"

"What?"

"You know. Living here in her palace all by herself. Wouldn't you get lonely?"

"If I lived in a palace I would. It's a pretty small palace."

"But it's all hers and it's — I don't know. I wonder if she's looking for another lover. Do you think she is, Hal?"

Impossible questions. That's what Tommie loved.

We met in college. She was at Pembroke and had a few classes over at Brown. One was a History of the Novel class, a real sleeper that met at eight in the morning. It was a good-sized sleeper with assigned seats. That was the Brown method of taking attendance. But most of us caught on pretty quickly that to our professors, a body was a body. If you were an early riser like my roommate Bobby Kahn, you could make a lot of money just by filling a chair. I paid him a dollar a class to sit in for me. That didn't even include the notes. Tommie paid her roommate Jeanne Ann Love seventy cents, notes included. Our first argument, Tommie's and mine, was about the discrepancy of wages in general, and what she paid Jeanne Ann in particular. I was a pretty good feminist, if anybody had called anybody a feminist back then. Tommie was definitely a capitalist. Equal pay for equal time, was my line. I was proud of that line. Until Jeanne Ann, who was listening, turned to Tommie and said, "Where does this guy get off?"

She was Tommie's bodyguard. Also her lover. That, we don't advertise. Almost every woman I knew in college, and this wasn't just the Bohemian bunch, was lovers with her roommate. That, we don't advertise either. And they all told me about it. I was their good ear. Brother Hal. I think a woman can spot a virgin, a male virgin, at a thousand paces. We're like open water to them, and out they steam, right into the middle of us, safe and sound, rocked like little babies.

Though I wasn't a virgin. There was my friend Danny in prep school. And one summer when I had a job rolling tennis courts, an older man named Leo. Tommie took it upon herself to initiate me into straight sex. That was sweet of her. She was ahead by two, or so she said. One would have been plenty. I was easily impressed. We borrowed Bobby Kahn's car and took some wine into the dunes on Cape Cod. She had her license, so she drove. I bought the wine because I looked older.

It's a beautiful place, Cape Cod. Sand, sea, sky. A good, simple place to lose your virginity. The best. We parked at the beach and walked for a while without saying much. Finally Tommie said, "Well, God. If we're nervous we should be, don't you think?"

It was late September. The summer people were gone, their cottages boarded up. Sweet cottages. White with aquamarine shutters, neat paths to the beach. The key hidden in the sand in front of the door. The thought crossed both our minds that it would be easier to love each other inside than out there naked in the dunes. We walked up to one of them and Tommie started digging. It took a few minutes but we found it, a glass jelly jar with a key inside.

The cottage we picked was smaller than the others. It sat close to the beach with two great big windows facing Spain. Portugal, said Tommie. Right. Portugal. There were two rooms, the one with windows which had a little wood stove, a rusty homemade thing that worked beautifully, given a little drift-wood, and a kitchen stocked with canned soups and crackers in tins and glass jars of pickles and something Tommie called me in to examine.

"It looks like a brain in brine," I said.

"You know what it is? It's pig's feet."

"Margaret?" I sometimes called her Margaret, which was her real name — Margaret Fair Thomas.

She pulled something from the back of a shelf. "Look, here's a ham!"

"Tommie? There's no beds."

Funny that a bed would be so hard to find in a house. What we came up with was sort of a Murphy thing in the window room. It pulled down from the wall like one of those hidden ironing boards, an unfortunate image that stayed with me. We made the bed up. There were plenty of blankets and a couple of old yellowed sheets. It was around midday, early afternoon. I said, "Do you want to go for another walk, or . . . " Tommie refused to finish the sentence for me. I was hungry, or said I was. We should have been. Breakfast had been hours ago, in the safety of Rhode Island. The question then was whether to trespass grandly, to steal flamboyantly, or to make such little dents in the stores as not to be noticed. That seemed boring to Tommie, a little prissy. "They won't be back until next summer. They'll never remember what was here and what wasn't. Let's eat the ham. Come on, Hal. Forget that stupid conscience of yours. If we find mustard, it was meant to be eaten. Agreed?"

A bit of a bully, that Tommie. I gave in to her. Cold ham with mustard and cranberry jelly. A can of Boston brown bread. The wine. We ate in the big room, looking out the windows. It was delicious.

At what point did it occur to us we could spend the night? Stay a week? Come back? This was our house now. Had I been anyone else, another male of my species, I might have looked around for something to repair. Tommie's reaction was female. She started to plan. "If we pace ourselves, the food will last two weeks, easily. Water might be a problem. But if they can turn it off, we can turn it on. There's got to be a valve somewhere."

"Tommie," I said. "We're students."

"So what? We're students. What makes you such a wet blanket? You're so nervous."

I looked at her and she knew. We both knew. She held out her hand and I took it, relieved. She moved very close to me. She put her arm around me, around my waist. There was a certain tension to it to remind me where we were going and who was leading. She started to unbutton my shirt and it was funny, I looked around for a shade to pull. "Relax," she said. "Don't be scared of me." She'd gotten her courage somewhere, maybe from the ham. "Can you relax, sweetie?" She laid me back on the bed. Had she ever seen me completely naked before? Yes, I think she had. I didn't have an erection. That worried me. She undressed quickly, not seductively. Businesslike. I said, "Tommie, what if I can't?"

"Can't what?" she said, to torture me I'm sure. Then she went to work. It was like watching a machine made for just such things — a warm, breathing, friendly machine. I looked at her body as she worked. I'd never seen her naked, not completely. I'd seen her breasts but not her crotch. Mostly I had the sight of her shoulder and her face in profile as she leaned over me and did as the others had, little Danny, Leo. This was different, but it felt good. It felt great.

After I came she moved up alongside me and draped her leg over both of mine, pressing my cock with her thigh. I grinned. "Do you think you could do that again?" I said.

"What we just did?"

"I liked it."

"Let's try this. A little different." She climbed onto me. Her breasts weren't large but they looked bigger hanging down. "Put your tongue on my nipple. That's it. That's nice. You can pull a little, like sucking. Oh, yeah. That's good. That's good." She had her eyes closed. I closed mine too. It was nicer that way. I could get into it more. She was moving, rocking on me, pressing my cock. I could feel it getting hard. "When it's ready, just put it inside me."

"Where?"

"You'll find it. Keep sucking my nipple."

And I did. I did find it, no problem. What happened in there felt good. Different from a mouth. But good. It was quick. I couldn't control anything and to this day I wonder what pleasure it could have been for Tommie. She was still moving when I was done and shrinking out of her, too much in my own world to worry about what to do next, how to touch her, how to make that thing happen to her that had just happened to me. Maybe she came. Women have different spasms, different noises. I wasn't much help to her, I know that.

We lay sweetly in each other's arms for a while, lazy and dozy.

Tommie said, "If we smoked, this is when we'd smoke."

I pressed my face against her hair. "I like you."

"I like you too."

"I think you're a good fuck."

"You say the nicest things."

We got up soon and dressed and left our house. I put out the fire and left a dollar in the kitchen with a note that said *Thanks for the ham.* Tommie was already outside, burying the key. We were quiet, peacefully so. We held hands along the beach and passed another couple holding hands, a man and a woman who nodded and smiled. It felt strange all of a sudden to have been recognized by them as one of them, when we were just Tommie and Hal, friends, not lovers, even after all that squirming around in the white cottage with the aquamarine shutters. I looked back and couldn't even tell which one was ours. They all had two windows. They all sat close to the beach. They all faced Portugal. Who were we kidding? But inside they were different, weren't they? They had to be. Inside was where people led their lives.

"What's the matter?" asked Tommie.

"Nothing. I was just thinking."

"Thinking about what?"

"Nothing."

"What besides nothing?"

"That bed."

"What about it?"

"Just how strange it was. The way it came out of the wall. Do you think all these other places have beds like that?"

"I'm sure they do. Look at them. The same person built them. They're all the same."

"Didn't ours seem smaller to you?"

"Not really."

"I think it was a little smaller."

We drove back to Providence and left the car at my dorm. I walked Tommie back to hers. We said good-bye outside in the dark. We kissed each other as we always did. It felt like it always did, just a little more solemn.

"Goodnight," she said.

"Goodnight."

"Hal? Are you going to be okay?"

"You mean about what? Today?"

"Today. Us. Everything."

"Yeah, I am."

Brighton

It turns out people at school think me and Maria are doing it.
How do I know? Helen tells me. She's cool about it. I go in to
visit and she says it's none of her business and she likes Maria,
she really does, but, like, if I'm not sleeping with her maybe I
should know everybody thinks I am. It's sort of a riot, she says.
Kids ask *me*.

What? If we're doing it?

Well, yeah.

So what do you say?

I say I hope you are.

Christ, Helen.

Only because I really like Maria, Brighty. She's cool. I think
I'd like to learn some of that karate stuff she does. I've seen her
practice. She's in the gym when we get there for basketball.
Man, you should see her kick. She can kick above my head,

easy! And she does this thing with a sword. She's all by herself in a corner with this sword, killing invisible people I guess. She's so, I don't know. She just doesn't let anything bother her. I wonder where she got a sword?

Sometimes me and Maria go to her house after school to listen to records and shit. Mr. DiAngelo's got these great records. This guy Puccini. All this fucking opera. I don't know why I never listened to opera before. Maria can't believe it. The first time she goes to put on Janis Joplin I tell her, hey, I know it's your house but I can't think with Janis Joplin. That's the point, she says. Turn off that little brain of yours. Relax a little. Take a break.

Maria doesn't do drugs. She says she doesn't because of the karate. It's not part of the karate way of life. Instead she listens to Janis Joplin. Sometimes the Mamas and the Papas, or the Doors, or Jefferson Airplane. I know all their names now because I see the albums lying around and their covers zap you. I think it's mind control but she says it's just good business.

I ask her if she's got any classical and she laughs. She says, sure. We've got Puccini. She shows me her dad's stuff, a great big stack. It's all Puccini. He owns a cement company and he seems like a pretty cool guy. I've never met him. I've met her mom, Mrs. DiAngelo. She's really short and she cooks a lot and sometimes she says things to Maria in Italian. She goes on and on and later I ask Maria, so what did she say?

Oh, just some dumb thing about the manicotti.

That's, like, some kind of pasta, isn't it?

Yeah, stuffed pasta.

So what's there to say about stuffed pasta?

Just that she likes you, you're a nice boy, and too bad you're not Italian.

Maria's got these headphones so she can listen to her stuff on her record player and I can listen to Puccini on Mr. DiAngelo's record player which is actually pretty feeble. I think maybe all it needs is a new needle. At first I'm afraid to play it really loud, the way it should be played. That's not a general rule or anything, but this particular music says loud to me. Mrs. DiAngelo's right around the corner in the kitchen, and I don't, you know, want to blast her. It's her house, isn't it? Finally she comes out and I'm kind of dancing around in the living room. Maria's dancing around in her room with the headphones on. That must be weird for a mom. Anyway, I don't see her right away and when I see her I'm really embarrassed. I go to turn down the music even though it's not on loud. I figure that's what she's here to tell me. I say, gee, Mrs. DiAngelo, I'm really sorry. My worst thought is that I've ruined the dinner or something, like some soufflé's fallen. That's what Mom used to tell us. Don't even breathe, the soufflé's in the oven. Then I remember Mrs. DiAngelo's not the soufflé type. I've had some of her food. She comes over to me, right next to me, and says, he's the great Puccini, isn't he? Yeah, I say, sure, he's really great. Well, she says, I have a problem with my ears in the kitchen. So if you could turn him up? Then she smiles and heads back to her stove.

After that we're, like, pals, Mrs. D. and me. We're the Puccini fan club. We never talk much. Her English isn't so great and I only know two words in Italian, *pasta* and *basta*. With her it's not about talking. I guess it's about music. Without the music on, we're a little uptight with each other. She has these ideas, maybe they're Italian. They're about men and how you treat them like they're really great, even if they're, like, seventeen years old and don't know what the fuck their life's about. It feels good to be treated that way, but it also makes me feel a little guilty. Like I don't deserve it. Maria says of course I don't deserve it. I don't have to. It's just something fucked-up in the Italian culture. I tell her I don't think it's all that fucked-up, really. Oh, she says, your true colors are showing. I knew it. Sooner or later the male chauvinist pig in all of you comes to the surface.

What's that supposed to mean?

Figure it out.

More of your fucking psychology?

What psychology? You're the one with the shrink. I don't know, Brighton, it's none of my business, it really isn't, but if you ask me, you're not any sicker than anyone else. You've got the same problems everyone else has.

Oh yeah? Then why doesn't everyone go to a shrink?

Money, stupid. Not everyone has parents who feel so guilty about their kid they'll pay to have some strange guy listen to him. That's all he does is listen, right?

He talks.

He should pay you then.

She waltzes into her room and slams the door, and I stand at the door and say, hey, Maria. She says, don't talk to me. Hey, I say. Look, let me in for a second. But she doesn't, and on the way home I think, wow, that was heavy. Male chauvinist pig. Wow. I guess that was our first fight.

I tell Pearlman me and Maria don't agree on a lot of superficial things. Like what? he says. Oh, like men and women and shit. You know, roles.

Oh, he says, superficial things like that.

And, well, we don't agree on you exactly. She thinks it's, like, dumb for me to come here and work on one part of my body when, um, the rest of it needs stuff too.

So you have different ideas about therapy.

Yeah. She thinks a person isn't just their head. A person is their heart too.

And?

Well, that's all.

How about their feet? Is a person their feet?

Well, no. I mean, no.

Why not? Why isn't a person their lungs? Right next to the heart, those lungs. Or their kidneys, Brighton. Or their balls.

He says this and I almost fall out of my chair.

Have you and Maria ever talked to each other about your relationship?

It's not a relationship. Man, I hate that word, relationship.

What would you call it?

We're friends.

So, a friendship?

Right.

Ever talked about it?

What's there to talk about?

Well, the things you like and don't like about each other. How it feels to be together. Whether you feel jealous of each other's friends.

We don't feel jealous. Why would we feel jealous? I don't have any other friends anyway.

And she doesn't either?

No, she does. She's got friends.

Do you spend time with them?

You mean, alone with them?

Alone or together. Do you socialize with them?

No, not really. They're all girls.

Girls, says Pearlman. He raises his eyebrows. But not girls you'd want to be friends with? Not like Maria?

They're, um, older.

Older?

Well, some of them are in college. Some of them don't go to college. The ones who work seem smarter than the ones in college. Or maybe they just know how to, like, talk to regular people. I don't think college necessarily teaches you how to communicate.

So you talk to them, to these young women?

They mostly talk to me.

Why, do you think?

Why do I think what?

Why do they talk to you when they could talk to each other?

I guess they have to. They talk to each other too.

They don't have to, says Pearlman. They want to.

Okay, they want to. They think they want to, but they don't even know me. Maybe they think I'm going to fall for them or something. I'm not going to fall for them.

I'm looking down at the rug, this plain brown rug. It looks like I end at the knees. I move my feet so I can see them. They look so big they look stupid. David says, falling for people isn't the most important thing.

Oh yeah? What is?

A lot of things are.

That's a horseshit kind of answer. What kind of answer is that?

He smiles. I should have seen it coming. I set myself up. He says, a horseshit kind of answer. He looks out the window and back again. See you next week.

Dad calls me in for a big talk. He calls it a powwow. That's weird. We never talk. Maybe he heard something about me and Maria and he, like, thinks it's time for that kind of talk.

We meet in the living room after supper. Helen's at basketball practice. Mom's there. That means it's not a sex talk. That's good. Dad starts with, gee, your sister's at basketball practice.

Yeah, I know. She's on the team and stuff.

Getting near the end of the season, says Dad.

It is, yeah.

I guess she's pretty coordinated, says Dad.

Uh-huh.

Well, we're proud of her, he says.

Is this, like, a talk about Helen?

It could be, couldn't it, says Mom. She gives Dad a look. She says, Bright, listen. I want to ask you something. Your father and I both do. Sit down, both of you. You make me nervous.

Sure, says Dad. He laughs like he's nervous. He sits down.

Mom says, what do you and your friends know about this war?

That's all? That's all you want to know? I look back and forth at them. They don't say anything. I say, well, I know where it is and I know, sort of, what it's about.

What's it about? says Mom.

Like, communism, I guess.

What about communism?

Well, you know. If we don't stop it there we'll have it here.

What do you think about that?

I think it's a bunch of bullshit. I look at Dad and say, I mean I think it's a really stupid idea. I think we've got enough problems in this country without going over there and fucking around with — I mean I think we should take care of our own problems first. That's all.

I can feel Dad getting ready to say something and I have this really strange thought. I think, what if he calls me son? It's funny. It's just a funny thought.

Mom says, so is this a war you want to fight?

I say, Mom, let's have Dad say something.

Uh, well, says Dad. He looks at the rug. This is really your mother's talk. We're concerned about the fact that you may be drafted into a problematic war you don't believe in, and we're wondering if you've explored your options.

Why is this Mom's talk? I say.

Well, only because she has strong opinions and I don't. You're almost eighteen. You're old enough to run your life. You can get out of the draft if you want to. You don't have to go fight anyone, you know that. You can go to college. I mean I assume you'll go to college and this won't be a problem anyway. Have you thought about college?

I, um.

I know you're just a junior, but the school must be getting some of you ready for applying to college.

I think college is kind of a dopey way out.

It's the smart way out, Brighton.

I think if I do anything, I'll do a c.o.

You may not get a c.o. I wouldn't count on it.

Then I'll go to Canada.

Brighton, says Mom, but Dad interrupts her. He says, oh yes, that makes a lot of sense. Run from your government. Live the fugitive life. Pal around with other fugitives. Live in a nice little town in Canada where people will love you and accept you because you refused to serve your country or take a simple way out. Well, I'm telling you, it doesn't work like that, son. Nobody wants a fugitive. Nobody wants to feed or house a draft dodger. Not even Canadians. These American kids think this war gives

[72]

them carte blanche to run anywhere they want and be accepted there. World citizens. Draining other people's resources, paying no taxes, living in communes —

Dad, I say, cool it. Then I turn around and leave the room.

I don't shoplift normally. I don't buy much stuff, to tell you the truth. Not records. Not clothes. I don't know where I get my clothes. Mom buys them I guess. I get shitty jobs in the summer, like lawns, which I don't actually mind because people leave you alone. If they don't, you can't hear them anyway. I like the sound of a mower. There was this one lady, pretty old and rich, with a lot of lawns, four big lawns. She liked me I think. Or else she was really bored. She used to come out with her lunch on a little plate, like a china plate, and wherever I was she'd find me and follow me around the whole time eating her little sandwiches. They were bite-sized sandwiches. One day she showed them to me. I didn't need to see them but she needed to show them to someone I guess. I understand that. She was a lonely lady. Some of them were pink inside, some of them were light green, some of them were yellow. She said she made them herself. Here's a lady with a thousand cooks and she made them herself. I told her they looked nice, they'd make a good picture, they looked really nice. Well, I guess no one ever said that to her before or seemed interested, because she started to cry. I was just paying attention to her, that's all. I was just the person who mowed her lawn and I was sort of letting her walk along with me. I don't think people need a whole lot, that's my philosophy. But it's funny, sometimes they'd rather get it from someone they pay.

So at the end of the summer I have some money. It lasts pretty much until the next summer. When it runs out I borrow from Helen. Miss Moneybags. Where do you get all your dough? I ask her. She says, I just don't spend it. Her jobs are things like baby-sitting, and in the summer she works at this old bowling alley, setting up the pins when people knock them down. It's candlepin bowling. The same guy owns a driving range and sometimes she works there, picking up golf balls at night.

I don't spend it either, I say. I don't buy anything. What do I buy?

Books.

She's right. I buy books. What else?

I don't know. Combs. I just bought a comb. Shampoo. Stuff like that. Food. Don't you ever buy food?

Sometimes I buy a Coke.

I buy food. I buy gum. I buy little notebooks, pens. Brighty, you must buy pens. I'm always buying little erasers and pens.

I never do.

What do you write with?

I don't know. Pens, I guess. But I don't buy them.

Where did you get them?

I just find them. Or I take them from Dad.

Helen gives me a look and I say, you eat their food don't you? You live in their house.

So?

So it's the same thing. It's like living in a commune. You share stuff.

I thought you hated communes.

She's right. I do. She's funny, Helen. What's funny is there she is, rolling in dough, and here I am, I never spend a cent, I use Mom's shampoo, I steal pens from Dad, I eat all their food, I sleep in their house, and I've got nothing. Maria says it makes sense. I say what do you mean it makes sense? She says, it makes sense, Brighton. The law of karma. What goes around comes around. It's in that book I gave you. It means if you spend more money you'll have more. That's when I decide to buy Mr. DiAngelo a needle.

I'm in this record store in the Forties, flipping through P for Puccini in this long aisle of opera. People are running everywhere but nobody's helping. They always run in New York. This is the kind of store that has big shoplifting problems I bet. When you can't find what you want, and you can't find someone to help you find it, if you're like me you think, well, why should I pay for it? It's just a dumb needle. No sweat. It's a discount place anyway. You take the needle, then take off the discount, then take off what you'd pay for the service you never got. Well, how much could this teeny thing cost?

The needle goes into my pocket and someone says, hello, Brighton. I look behind me for the other Brighton. Then I look and see this person I've never seen before and I say, me? He says, is there another Brighton? And by then I recognize Hal. I can't explain it. It's just one of those weird things that happen when you meet a person you know in a place you've never seen them before. Once that happened to me with Dad in a bathroom in the airport. Pretty recently. It was the Newark Airport. We were, like, side by side at the urinals and even though that's not a place where you're looking the other guy in the face, you can still sort of feel who's next to you. Or I can. Usually. I forget why he was there. I mean at the airport. Maybe he went on a business trip or something. I was there to pick him up and they said his plane wasn't in yet. We both went to the sink and I looked and saw him in the mirror and for a few seconds I didn't know who it was. I just thought it was some guy, old enough to be my dad, some decent looking, sort of sad and tired looking guy. He said, Brighton? like it was a question. I said something dumb like, Dad, gee, you got here. How was your trip? Dumb. It was embarrassing.

Sometimes I think about how in certain parts of the world, like in Vietnam, the survivors have to go into the rubble and identify the bodies of their family, and I think how really bad that would be, like really cruel, because here they are alive and the rest are dead, plus they have to look at every single body in there, even if the head's gone or there's just a couple of legs left, and they have to remember at a time like that what their father or their sister really looked like. And naked. And with gory wounds and shit. Man, if there's one thing I learned from meeting Dad in the bathroom, and meeting Hal Chapin in the record store, it's how much we don't pay attention. Half the time we don't see what we're looking at. More than half. Even when we do, we don't remember it. Basically, we're just looking at ourselves.

Hal's wearing this three-piece suit, a flowered tie and a raincoat. How are you? he says. Usually when people say this they don't mean it, but he waits for me to say something and when I don't he says, are you all right?

Uh, yeah. I . . . well. I'm just nervous. When I meet someone by surprise I get kind of nervous.

Me too.

I, uh, well. So. What are you doing here?

Verdi.

You mean you're buying something?

That's why I come here. To buy things. What are you up to?

Oh, well, I'm buying something too.

He looks and sees I'm in the P's. Puccini, he says. I didn't know you were an opera buff, Brighty. It's funny he calls me Brighty. Only really Helen calls me that.

I'm not, I say. I mean I'm just starting. There's this girl I

know, and me and her mother, well, we listen to Puccini sometimes in the afternoon. It sounds kind of strange.

Not really. My mother's a great Wagner fan. But she wouldn't
touch Puccini. In my experience, most women, most mothers,
prefer Wagner. Why do you think that is?

You're asking me? I've never even listened to Wagner. How
do you say his name again?

Like Vagner, with a *v*.

He's got his Verdi and I've got my needle in my pocket. We
start walking to the front and he says, didn't you want to buy
something?

Oh, I, um. No. Not today. I'll come back.

Because I can pay for it if you don't have the money on you.
You can just owe me.

I figure he's been talking to Helen, that bigmouth, who tells
him she's lending me money. No, it's okay, I say. I didn't really
want anything anyway. I'm just, you know, window-shopping.

I should have said shoplifting, but I didn't. Maria says that's
when I ended up on the wrong side of the law of karma. We get
in line at the cash register and I say, I'm pretty much not very
generous. I don't think that's good, I think it's a flaw.

Maybe you're just careful, says Hal.

The line's pretty slow. I say something about it and Hal says,
the great thing about standing in line is you can pretend you're a
Russian housewife and this is your whole life.

Why's that great?

It's not. It's awful. But it teaches compassion.

I tell him about the book I'm reading, the one on Buddhism.
It's all about compassion.

I've read that book, he says.

You're kidding? I mean, I'm surprised. It's not even a library
book or anything.

He laughs. I had to read it in school, when I was in college. That was my minor, Eastern religions.

No shit. Wow. I didn't even know they had courses like that back then. I mean it's pretty far out stuff, isn't it? I mean, no offense.

He laughs again. We're at the register now and suddenly I think, what am I doing here? I'm not buying anything. Then I remember he's the one buying something. She's got it all totaled up, this young, sort of pretty I guess, girl. She turns to me and I say, no, I'm with him. We start walking out of the store. He's got his records in a bag and I'm walking behind him watching the bag, wishing the damn needle was in the bag and all paid for instead of stolen and in my pocket. We're almost out the door when suddenly this guard, this police-type guy, comes from nowhere and steps in front of me and Hal. He's more in front of Hal and I don't think he has to do this, I mean it's not part of his job, but he has this little club, like a billy club but shorter, and he sticks it right up against Hal's face. It's touching his face. He says, stop right there. Hal says, I don't think we're going anywhere, are we, Brighton? But I can't say a word. Hal says, you can remove your stick, officer. We're not armed and we're not dangerous and we're not going anywhere and this record is paid for. But the guy doesn't move the stick. He keeps it in Hal's face and he starts frisking him with the other hand. Some people in the store are sort of staring at us but most of them don't give a shit. They've seen it all, these New Yorkers. The guy's frisking Hal's pants now and Hal says something I don't hear but I can tell he's losing it. The guy straightens up and says right in Hal's face, I don't know if I heard that right. Say that one more time. Say it! That's when I lose it. I go for him right at the knees and I deck him. I fucking deck the guy.

I learned something. I learned that when I'm really pissed off I can fight, and when I fight the whole world goes away. It's like it disappears through a hole in the ground. I could die and not know it. I could die and not even care about it. That's what happens with soldiers. I understand it now.

I don't remember anything except Hal pulling me out of there, out the door and onto the sidewalk to cool off. Someone else must have pulled the police guy somewhere else. Hal tells me later it was a quick fight, really intense, really silent and scary. That's probably the only way I can ever fight. I have to get in a kind of trance. Like a mongoose, says Hal.

We're sitting on the train. I've got his handkerchief over my eye. That's where I got cut by the guy's billy club. Not a deep cut. Still, it's bloody and I'm ruining the handkerchief. I'll get you a new one, I say.

Don't bother. I've seen the way you shop.

No, I will. I'll get you a new one.

I lean against the window and rest. Hal says, I bet some ice would feel good on that eye.

It would, yeah.

He goes to the Club Car and gets the ice and makes a little ice pack with the handkerchief. Do you know how lucky we are? he says. We were very lucky.

It turns out the guard was on his first day of work and he was really out of line with that billy club. He's not supposed to carry a weapon. In a record store? Are you kidding? Whoever saw me stick the needle in my pocket must've passed the word up to him, and this was his first day and he was excited. I understand that. But he had no business treating Hal the way he did, basically like a piece of shit, when it was me who stole the needle. Some higher-up who was a friend of Hal's saw the fight, and in the end the guard got a warning. I got a warning too, from Hal, for shoplifting, even though I pretended I forgot the needle was in my pocket. The higher-up pretended he believed me. Hal didn't pretend anything. He just went and paid for it. It cost, like, less than a dollar.

What was that guy's name? I say.

Which guy?

The higher-up. Your friend.

That's Bobby Kahn. We were roommates in college.

Does Mom know him?

She knows him well. She drove his car to Cape Cod and back with me in it.

Is he, like, the kind of person to call her up and tell her what happened?

Someone's got to tell her. What's she supposed to think, your shrink gave you a black eye?

How do you know I go to a shrink?

You're right. He looks down at his lap. It's none of my business.

Just how do you know, that's all. I'm not mad or anything. It's not really that private. Helen told you, right? It's okay if she did. She's got a big mouth, but I like Helen.

She likes you.

We didn't ever really fight when we were kids, but we didn't really get along either. I don't think you can get along unless you fight. I didn't get along with anybody I guess.

You sure didn't get along with me. You didn't like me at all.

He's right. I think of him in a bathing suit, with rolls of fat, the way he was when we first moved in next door. I didn't like him. Helen liked him. Mom did. I thought enough people liked him, so I didn't. That's a crappy reason for anything.

Hal

Helen and I shared a confidence that struck everybody but us as very odd. Frank probably thought I was molesting her, but Tommie knew I was only brainwashing her. That's a joke. What I was doing was listening to her. I've never met a kid, and it's true, I haven't met all that many, but a kid so good with people, so in the know. She wasn't clever. That's exactly what she wasn't. She was the most sincere thing to come down the pike since, I don't know when. Since I did, I guess. That's one thing I used to be and lost along the way and found in her, a killing sincerity.

I wanted to protect her from what lay ahead. I always felt very maternal towards Helen, anyone could see that. Right from the start, the day I first met her. We horsed around in the pool together and I guess we just fell in love. She was maybe five years old. I was a boy of thirty.

She could be snippy, but only when she felt threatened. Jody threatened her. Erica didn't. That's what I mean, she had radar for what was important. I remember one time, in the gap between Erica and Jody, when a guy called Dennis, your basic con man, stayed at my house for a few weeks, having sex with me and hiding from his wife. At the time I didn't know he was hiding from his wife. Maybe it wouldn't have made any difference. He was a man I'd met in a bar, a black cave of a place with a stingy dance floor and a few tables. Salt and pepper shakers shaped like cocks. If you tried hard enough and were as starved as I was after thirty-eight years in the closet, you could, in that dimness, just make out the ratty posters that papered the walls and even the ceiling: huge, glossy erections, both black and white, dubiously attached to real human beings. A decor designed to get us out of there and home with each other as fast as possible, or out into an alley at least. Unlike so many of the Village bars in the sixties, before Stonewall, the prissy places that were more like being at a tea party than at a bar. Endless, pre-sexual conversation, slow inebriation, a sense of propriety. Later I found those haunts. That's where I met Jody. But in the beginning I needed an impersonal darkness in which to carry out this business of getting to know myself.

Dennis looked like a god. Out of the bar and into the street, I looked at him and saw what a catch I'd made. He spent his days in a gym somewhere while his wife (I learned this later) went to work. He was "looking for work," that was his story. His story to her and later, briefly, to me. The autobiography of Dennis M.

What did I know about gods? The temple at Delphi should have tipped me off, with its *Know Thyself* carved in stone. If Dennis fell short of that, I did too. I had no idea you could just walk in, celebrate the flesh, and be on your way again. It was good and right to be mortal, to be profane. I stopped by his table. He was sitting alone. He was off-duty, that was my first impression. He looked like someone who knew how to pose and was done for the night. I was wrong about that. I sat down and said, "Hi. Can I join you?" He looked off to the side, towards the door. I said, "Oh, you're waiting for someone. Sorry," and got up to go.

"No, they're not coming," he said. "If he's not here now, he's not coming. This guy. Just a friend. What's your name?"

"Hal."

"Nice to meet you, Hal. I'm Dennis."

I was used to this now, getting used to it. Hi, I'm so-and-so. Never a last name. Never a handshake. Make eye contact instead. "Can I buy you something?" I said. "A drink?"

"Yeah. Great."

"What are you drinking?"

"This thing's a Manhattan."

"You want another one of those?"

"I guess. Yeah. This guy was buying. I never had one before."

"This is the right place for it."

"You think they're good here?"

"Well, no. I mean I've never had one here. I meant, uh, Manhattan. The place."

"Oh, yeah," he grinned. "I get it. Sure, Manhattan."

I went off to buy the drinks and had my chance to escape but didn't take it. Instead, I gave myself a pep talk. Remember, the who doesn't matter. The who can be anyone. Keep your eye on the prize. Keep the end in sight. That a way, Hal. I got back to the table and Dennis was right in the middle of a yawn. "So," he said. "I've never seen you in here before. You come here a lot?"

"Not a lot. Sometimes. I think I've seen you before." That was an outright lie on my part.

"You sure it was me? I'm not in here much."

"Maybe not. Is there somebody else who looks like you?"

Questions like this were usually for my own entertainment, but Dennis plowed through, and I began to see something in him I could be attracted to, besides his godlike looks which were only vaguely evident in the light of the cave. He said, "You won't believe this but I've got a twin brother."

"No kidding?"

"Identical twins. We still look alike and everything. We dress pretty different. That's about the only way you can tell us apart. I guess I dress the way he dresses on weekends."

It was hard to imagine a straight-arrow brother dressing like Dennis dressed, even on weekends. He was wearing a black T-shirt and a pair of tight black dungarees. By tight I mean tight, all those hours in the gym. He'd ripped the sleeves off the T-shirt to show off his biceps. A bit of overkill. I said, "Maybe it was your brother. He comes in here too?"

"This place?" Dennis laughed. He shook his head. "That'll be the day."

We drank our drinks, looking off in opposite directions. It was early, still dead. I'd come straight from work and felt con-spicuously overdressed, suddenly inadequate in terms of small talk. Usually what happened was after a few drinks with a man, I'd let him feel me up while I sat there torn between guilt and explosion. Or we'd grope around mutually, but even then I was somewhere up on the ceiling, looking down on us like a sports-caster or a weatherman. *Chapin hits a line drive to left field. Tomorrow's forecast: fair, becoming partly cloudy with showers in the evening.* Shut up, Hal! I'd scream to myself, while in another world, miles away, a hand stroked my thigh or squeezed my cock with irrelevant urgency.

Dennis said, "So, what do you do?" He had a thin, almost whiny voice. Hard to believe it came from a body like his.

"I'm a buyer. I work for a clothing store. How about you?"

"Oh. Nothing right now. I'm looking for work. You live here? In the city?"

"No. In Jersey." I'd learned to say "Jersey" in places like this.

"Your own place?"

"Yeah."

"You live there alone?"

"Just me."

"Hey, that's nice. This city's . . . Well, it's fucked-up."

"I think it's all right."

"You don't live here, that's why."

"You're in the city?"

"Yeah. West Side. Thirty-eighth."

"Hell's Kitchen."

"You know it?"

"I grew up here."

Another pause. I watched two men come in, sit at the bar and begin to make out. Dennis drained his Manhattan and I went off to buy us another one. It felt good to be moving. Good to be standing there at the bar in the aura of something sexual and animal. The two men stopped for a moment to shed their jackets. One was my age and the other was younger by about twenty years. A kid. He had a pretty face, Italian or Greek. The older one might have been Irish. He was thick and red-haired and commanding. Yet seedy looking. Pathetic. Worried about a million things. I paid for the drinks and took them back to the table. I sat down. Dennis nodded. What was different? I felt gently drunk, a little sloppy, nothing new. But suddenly pressed for time. I took his hand across the table. I covered his hand with mine and pulled it towards me, leading him. Then leaning over sloppily, yet accurately, I covered his mouth with mine and thrust my tongue in and let it loll around, pull back, dart in and out, then slow down, lazy again, sucking from our kiss all that warm salty saliva. Interesting. Interesting? No, don't get caught in that, Hal. The kiss of death. Dive in again. Stay inside him. Hands on his face, the table no longer a solid object between us but a bed for my arms. I pulled his face closer, down into me, begging this anchor of human touch to keep me from floating up and away, out of myself. And it did. Miracle of miracles. It held.

There was only one place to go after that. He said he had a roommate, a woman. A one-bedroom walk-up and he slept on the pull-out couch in the living room. I had a palace. We caught the subway to the tube, the tube to the train, the train to my car. Transportation as foreplay. I made a joke to myself and laughed and he said, "What?" but I couldn't explain it, or bear to have the explanation misunderstood. Don't think about his mind, Hal, take in his body. In the car on the way home from the station I stopped twice, once in a parking lot behind a bank and the second time right by the road, to put my hands on him. He let me. Don't let him speak, I thought. Oh, God, don't give me your voice. I kissed him hard and long, right at the source of language. Not a word.

I don't know what makes us good or bad in bed. I think it has everything to do with chemistry. For me it does. But Dennis, and others I've met, could make love well to anything. Anyone. I didn't know this about him until we undressed, I just knew what I felt. In fact I assumed he was shy and, despite the physique, inexpert.

His cock went off at an angle, that was the first thing I noticed. We stood on opposite sides of the bed, facing each other, and I flicked the light off. "Leave it on," he said. No longer the whiny voice. A different voice, hard as marble. "Now look at me." He took his cock and stroked it, keeping his palm flat under it, stroking it like it meant nothing to him. "Come over here." I started to walk around the bed, then for some reason climbed over it. I slid across the sheets like the thin, athletic man I wasn't. It could have been disastrous. Instead it was my first experience of bodily grace linked to sex.

Later, pushing into him, it was there again for me. The bunched muscles of his slightly arched back, his taut buttocks, the backs of his thighs pushing against the front of mine. His body seemed to make mine more beautiful, more right and at ease in a way it never had been before. It was his doing. I had thought I would run the fuck, prove something and let him go. But he ran it. He was truly a body. He lived there in his body in a way I never had.

The next day was a Friday and I didn't go to work. I called and told them I had a head cold. That weekend we got up only to make coffee, and I think we ate a sandwich at one point. I really don't remember.

Sunday night, about eight o'clock, Helen came over. I never locked the house and she knew just to walk in. Possibly she knocked but I didn't hear it. So when I came downstairs in my bathrobe to fix a plate of cheese and crackers, a glass of wine for me, a beer for Dennis, and found her there in the kitchen eating potato chips and thumbing through *Vogue*, I was surprised. I was shocked. She represented another life, a Hal temporarily abandoned, and to meet it there in the kitchen without warning, well, I felt doused with cold water. I yelled at her. It was a stupid thing to do.

"What are you doing here? When did you get here?" The truth was I was afraid of what she'd heard coming from my bedroom.

"Oh, cool it," was all she said, sounding like her brother. She flipped the magazine at me and hopped off her stool.

"I'm just surprised. I didn't hear you come in."

"Don't worry. I'm on my way out."

She left. I didn't try and stop her. Both our feelings were hurt. I knew she knew everything. The minute I yelled at her she knew. She probably even knew his name.

I didn't see her again until the day I finally got him out of there. After our paths crossed in the kitchen, I went back upstairs and knew I needed to cry. I thought it would be possible to cry in Dennis's arms. I went in to him fully expecting that.

"Where's the food?" he said.

"I forgot it."

"Man, I'm starving." I climbed in next to him. "Who was down there?"

"A friend of mine. My friend Helen."

"I thought it was a cat you were yelling at. Who's Helen?"

"She lives next door. She's just a kid."

I could feel the untruth of the words as I said them. But Helen wasn't a conversation I could have with Dennis. Nothing was. We couldn't speak, I already knew that about us. We could only touch. Or maybe we could only fuck. I took his arm and wrapped it around me and tucked myself against him. But he didn't understand. He pulled himself away and got up.

"Man, I'm dizzy. I'm seeing stars." He sat down on the bed. "Let's eat something. I gotta eat."

We ate, and didn't make love again that night. He fell deeply asleep. He snored, something I wasn't prepared for. In the morning I said I was going to work, expecting he'd go into the city with me and we'd part at Gimbel's, make a plan for next weekend. But instead he said, "I'll take you to the station. That way I can use the car."

I don't know what he did with his days. He had a con man's sense of timing, and made dinner for me the first night, a candlelit affair, our first real meal together. The candles, it turned out, were there to disguise the poverty of what lay on our plates, shoe leather pork chops taken from my freezer. The next night he dropped the pretense and prepared a fried egg sandwich for each of us.

You don't bring a man home and put him to work for you, make him your kitchen slave, I know that. Not on the first date. But most people don't bring a man like Dennis home, period. Or they bring him home and send him home. Why not you, Hal Chapin? I was afraid I'd never have sex like that again, that's why. I was afraid I'd never again fuck my brains out, afraid I'd go back to my place on the ceiling, hovering over the sex act. So I let one day roll into the next. And I enjoyed our time in bed. We were fine as long as we didn't talk. I gave him money every morning and he shopped for dinner, which I made. I'd come home to find a wilted lettuce and half a pound of hamburger. Why didn't I care where the rest of it went? That two and two didn't make ten?

One day, out of the blue, he said he was looking for work.

"Here?" I asked him.

"In the area."

"You want to give up your life in the city?"

"What life? You don't think it's such a good idea, I can tell."

"No, I'm just surprised. I mean, you've got an apartment there, friends, I don't know. I don't know much about you, I guess. I mean about who you are."

"What's the matter with who I am?"

"Nothing. Nothing's the matter with it."

"I don't get it. I tell you I'm looking for work and you get on some weird trip about it. Like I'm moving in with you. I'm not moving in with you. All I need is a week. One more week. Not even. Just until I find a job. It's gonna happen, I can feel it."

Like all good con men, he knew my thoughts before I knew them myself. He prepared the ground and I planted myself in it and came up gullible as a weed. I don't know how his wife found me, unless she traced a phone call somehow. During dinner one night the phone rang. I got up to answer it. "Hello," she said. It was a polite voice. God knows why it was, but it was. "You don't know me, but I know who you are and I know my husband is there with you. May I please speak to him?" Without a word I brought the phone to the table. Dennis went white, then red. He took the receiver and slammed it down into the cradle. That night I put him on a train.

The next morning I was upstairs shaving when I heard the front door open and close. Christ, he's back, I thought. I went to the top of the stairs, divided by shaving cream, Janus-like, brandishing the razor.

"Hi," said Helen. "He's gone, right?"

I nodded.

"When did he go?"

"You tell me, Sherlock."

"I think he went yesterday."

"He went last night."

"That's what I thought. Hal? I didn't like him."

"I know that."

"I thought he was stealing from you, that's why. You don't have to say if he was or he wasn't, but that's why."

"Thanks."

We stood looking at each other for a long minute. This was something we were good at. We'd never found it hard. Finally she said, "Well, I have to go to school now."

"You better go."

"You're not good at math, right?"

"What kind of math?"

"This thing called factoring out."

"I'm good at it. I'm great at it."

"Have you ever heard of it?"

"No, but bring it over. We'll take a look at it."

"Tonight?"

"Fine."

"Okay, see you," she said, and ran.

I always had to be careful not to wish her never to change. One day she was a fish in my pool, the next she was an antelope leaving my house.

PART TWO

Tommie

The swan turns forty. I can't stand it. Why Hal wants to celebrate is beyond me. Fete yourself, I tell him. Yours is soon enough. Vulture, hyena, carrion crow sitting on a fence singing *hey dee diddle oh I owe you.*

The guest list causes actual pain. Will cause. I prepare myself. After supper I lift my carcass from the chair, wish them farewell, rehearse my eventual death, but do it with a sense of humor. Go into the living room and sit down with a legal pad and pencil. Nothing comes. One name comes. The blankness is intimidating. Go to the kitchen. No one. Nothing left of my family. The table is cleared. Make myself a hot gin and back to the living room. Speak to me, angels. Who the hell are my friends?

"This is not a guest list," says Hal. "This is an insult, Tommie. To yourself." Saturday noon and I've dragged myself over. They are just getting up. When was the last time I had sex in the morning? Late Jurassic?

"Give it here," says the weasel. He is a weasel, that Jody. The men men choose for lovers. Appalling. Eyes that never land anywhere. Dark hair slicked back with something putrid. The mess on the pillow in the morning. I give up. "Oh," says the weasel, glancing at the legal pad. He giggles. "Oh, dear."

"Have you eaten?" says Hal. I know he loves me.

"I'm not hungry, thank you. I'm a breatharian."

"Eat with us. Jody, get another chair from the dining room."

Weasel frowns. "Bossy, bossy, bossy."

The second he's out of the room I say, "How can you stand it, darling?"

"Stand what?"

"Married life."

"You just stand it."

He comes back in and we sit down to eat eggs Florentine. Apropos of nothing, Weasel says, "No, seriously. My sister's one."

"One?" I stare at him.

"A breatharian."

"I'm happy for you."

"She cheats though. Sometimes she eats grass and flowers."

"Grass and flowers, well. She's a *carpe diem* kind of gal, isn't she? No will power, that's her problem. What about eating out?"

"She'll order a salad. Sometimes she eats fish and chicken, but only if it's cooked a certain way. She doesn't eat cream sauces. Too much milk. And nothing flambéd."

"All that booze. Tut tut."

"She drinks booze, she just doesn't like to eat it."

"She's not a Mormon, is she?"

"I don't think so."

"Not more than one wife?"

"She's not even married."

"I like this sister of yours. Let's have her for dinner. Hal will cook. She'll eat veal, won't she?"

"Veal?"

"Most breatharians eat veal."

"I guess she'll eat almost anything if you put it in front of her."

"We'll be sure and put it in front of her. It'll be fun, Hal. What do you say?"

"Behave, Tommie," is what he says, "or I'll have to send you home."

Jeanne Ann Love's is the only name on the guest list. Hal uncorks a bottle of champagne and slowly, dram by dram, the other names pile up after her. People I don't know. People I don't want to know. Friends of Hal's, some of whom I know. Friends of Weasel's, oh spare us. Weasel's sister. Bobby Kahn. Hal suggests David Pearlman. "Nix on that," I say. "He'd come in wearing all my money."

"I meant he could cater it," says Hal. "Just kidding, just kidding."

"I think we need some more females," says the weasel.

"Oh my," I say. "Perspicacity's in our midst."

"Tommie, shut up," says Hal.

"Be nithe," says the weasel.

We set our minds to more females. Helen's fourth grade teacher, Brighton's English teacher. We're grasping. Frank's secretary. The butcher's wife. Hal stops us there. He points the champagne bottle at me. "Where have you been?"

"It's sad, isn't it?"

"It's unbelievable. Who do you talk to?"

"You."

"Besides me."

"Not a soul, I promise."

"It's pitiful, Tommie."

"Oh, come on. It's life."

"It's not life. It was never your life in college. You had a thousand friends."

"*You* had a thousand friends. I had two friends, one of whom is now my neighbor and phone pal. That's not so bad, fifty percent. Anyway, of all your thousands, who do you talk to besides me?"

"I saw Bobby Kahn the other day."

"Doesn't count."

"I've outgrown them. We're in different worlds."

"Well, there."

"But I've made new ones, darling. This is the point."

"Sure you have. Helen's your friend. Now Brighton's interested. Stealing my children. And then of course you have your sex friends. You have your lovers. If I could get out from under, believe me, I would. I'd do just what you're doing. I'd fuck anyone, anywhere. I'd even fuck men. I'd lie to Frank. I already do by being married to him. But the others. My two little ones. Little — Christ! What year is this champagne? Children. Do you have any children, Weasel?" Apparently he doesn't know his name. "If you ever have any, you and Hal, keep them with you at all times. Tie them to the house. You got that?"

"Why do we have to listen to this bullshit?" he says to Hal.

"One simple reason," I say. "I got here first."

Erica's name goes on the guest list because we're hoping Frank will run off with her. If I have a God it's this: Second Chances.

Hal is hopelessly sentimental, wants to know where she'll sleep. "With you, darling. Where else? You're the one with the motel."

"She can't stay here, Tommie. Not with Jody."

"Not in your bed, stupid. Under your bed."

Jeanne Ann, we decide, will stay chez moi, and the rest who don't haul themselves home afterwards will probably sleep where they fall. The breatharian sister and boyfriend will come up from Delaware to honor her — what shall we call me? — her brother's husband's wife. Hal is having the pool cleaned. My own Helen painted it. A troop of grown-up boy scouts comes in to do the lawn and hedges. Then a gang of stevedores to raise a tent, enormous fluffy thing on his back forty. This will be a gay event. The caterers are two Frenchmen, Hal's pals. Fine, I say, as long as they keep their clothes on this time. There was a party once, I was there and they catered it, one of Hal's parties, where these two, one black, one white, wearing tiny aprons and nothing else, balls to the breeze, bounced from guest to guest offering canapés and champagne.

"Clothes on?" says Hal. The lady doth protest. "Tommie, be reasonable."

If I am anything, I am reasonable. Have become so. Am made insane by it. It was always Frank's thing, steady and reasonable, the man thing. Then Brighton arrived, scrawny, wet, helpless, such a little animal, and my breasts ached for him. Out of nowhere. I remember the moment. I knew I would throw myself in front of a train to save his life, this ugly baby, just because he made my breasts ache. He was the first person in the world I knew I would die for.

Faith came and went, a breezy sort of spirit. A heart that never woke up. The minute I laid eyes on her (thank God I was awake for those few hours she lived), I could see something wrong, that she was terribly homesick, and I thought, oh Baby, if this is how it feels already, you won't be long with us, will you? We didn't name her until after she died. That changed everything, her death. The train I would throw myself in front of to save my child's life, came invisibly. I must have turned to watch a crow fly, or a shadow, and in that moment of inattention she was gone. To survive such things a person becomes reasonable. At first. Later, when everyone's safely grown up and there's more time, we go crazy with grief.

Brighton says, "I'd like to talk to you, Mom, about something. Okay?"

"Okay."

"Can we go somewhere?"

"Somewhere like where?"

"Just not in the house. In the car somewhere. I'll drive you."

He isn't the world's best driver, my son. For that reason alone I don't look forward to this. Add a lecture to it, or a confession, and it promises to be a long afternoon. "Wait," I say. "I'll powder my nose."

"Oh, Mom."

The impatience of youth, and a sleuth for a son who knows I don't powder anything, never have and never will. Don't even know how to. Wonder if it's a girl he wants to tell me about. Never thought of that until this minute. Oh God, Tommie, forty creepeth up fast. I steal cash from Frank's top bureau drawer. Lunch money. So endearing, must reach down through the socks and boxers, digging for dollars. We go in the Volvo, Frank's car. I hate this car. On the way out I wave at the stevedores raising my tent. "See the tent, Brighton?"

"What's it for?"

"My party."

"Already?"

"Already is tomorrow, boy-o."

"Mom. Don't call me that."

"Turn left," I say at the bottom of the driveway, anxious to control my own destiny, joke of jokes. In tiny increments it's possible, but in the end it all adds up to jackshit, excusez-moi le français. I'm cranky today. I sat up late with Hal last night. Jody, as I'm meant to call him now, had gone to bed. We were nit-picking the last fussy details. Fag work. Something Hal excels at, but me, I'm hopeless. Nothing to do but keep us oiled and remind him who taught him to make a martini.

"I never drink martinis, Tommie."

"Did I say drink? I said make. Vive la différence."

He was sipping wine, of all prehistoric things, and I'd mixed my gin with vermouth for a change, vermouth and a twist of lemon. I don't do the hot milk combination in public, not even in front of Hal. Let's call it the only secret I have from him, or almost.

"Have you heard from her?" he asked.

"No."

"Where did you send the invitation?"

"Where else would I send the invitation? Snakeshit, Pennsylvania."

"Sockshoot. It's an Indian name."

"Indian name, my ass. It's what white people do for fun."

"What? Shoot socks?"

"Make up Indian names."

"Bored white people."

"We're born bored."

"I wasn't. I was born bald."

"What do you think people do in Snakeshit, P.A.?"

"I only know one person and she teaches chemistry."

"They must be very busy there in good old Snakeshit. Promoting themselves. The Chamber of Commerce. *If you lived in Snakeshit you'd be home now! Stay a while in Snakeshit. Snakeshit: Over Fifty Beds. Home of Jeanne Ann Love.* Why the fuck doesn't she get in touch with me, Hal?"

"The sour note you parted on, perhaps?"

"Oh, stop being so obvious. We smoked pot together in this house, if you remember. Since then."

"And that healed what?"

"Forgive me, Father. You're talking like a fucking priest."

"Why not? You could use one."

"Speak for yourself."

"All right. I could use one too. A handsome seminarian. Or an acolyte if I have a choice."

"You have no choice. Your choice is upstairs asleep, dearie."

"You have such a bitter root, Tommie."

"Plumbum."

We are whizzing along, my son and I, my grown-up baby son. I'm tempted to tell him the truth, that nothing he can do or say can shock me after that first shock of seeing the size of his infant balls, the balls he came in with, a wrinkled magenta fruit, plum size, enormous, dwarfing his tiny whip of a penis. They knocked me out for that birth and as I came to he was held out to me, the dark fruit between his legs like nothing I had ever imagined. It terrified me. No, it startled me first, then I became frightened. A woman doesn't say these things. She smiles and says *coo coo,* and when they leave her alone with him for the first time she gives him her nipple and weeps.

With him and Helen both there was a certain terror, not the new mom terror of *will I drop it and give it brain damage?* but a more enduring deep uneasiness about bodies. Bodies and touch. Bodies and touch and maternal responsibility. I was there to give tit — lord, what language, Tommie — and wipe bottoms. (Something so unjovial about revisiting one's own breast milk on its way out, transformed into smelly mustard paste.) To nurse was my idea, all mine. The era discouraged it. It meant flapping a bosom in public, possibly, or wetting the front of a blouse whenever the hormones jumped. Frank liked it. His mother did not. My mother watched from heaven and thought her thoughts but kept them to herself. I had my response ready in case she visited me in a dream. It went like this: But Mother, I like to be sucked. These were not the problems. Other people were not the problem. The little mouth on my body felt good, it felt fine, but where I worried deeply, and where I hesitated, and where I may be guilty of ruining my children, was on the changing table or in the bath. I wasn't comfortable exploring their private parts, looking for early signs of rash or whatever mothers look for on their babies, as if they're objects they own which they do, someone has to, for the first bit at least, while they're still helpless on their backs. I didn't trust my instincts. What did I think? I'd fondle them and not know it, or not be able to stop myself? Those things weren't talked about. I assumed I was the only one in that dilemma, and maybe I was. One day, changing Brighton after a particularly messy diaper, I became conscious of the weight of something in my hand, his balls. I couldn't continue. I couldn't let go of them. I didn't like what held me there. It was a side of myself I was afraid to meet. He peed in my face, luckily, one of those direct hits coming from a little baby boy erection, and I — we — moved on.

"Mom," he says. "There's this, um, girl. Her name is Maria. Her last name is DiAngelo. She's Italian. I guess that's obvious. She's a senior."

I love this part, where the big wise mom gets to sit back in her seat and witness the unfolding of her son. I want to say to him, "Bright. Do you know what's happening here? You're joining the human race, you're doing your rite of passage right here in front of me in the front seat of your father's Volvo on our way to find a sandwich. I love you," I want to tell him. "I give you to her. I let you go completely." But I say nothing because I know better. I don't believe it. Not his end of the story and not mine. He doesn't love this girl. He'll never love her. She's just practice. And even so, am I not jealous? I am jealous. And do I let him go completely? I am a mother, not a fool.

"That's wonderful," I say, and start to laugh.

He doesn't look at me, he looks ahead at the road. "What is?"

"Your new friend."

"Why are you laughing?"

"I'm not laughing at you, I'm laughing at me. Tell me about her. What else about her, this Maria of the angels?"

"That's incredible. How did you know that? That's just what I call her."

He with his heart on his sleeve. I bite my tongue and remind myself I'm the grown-up here, I'm still the grown-up, and to have this conversation with my changed and changing son should not be like luring a deer to its death, but to water and pasture. "Oh," I say, "I knew some Italian in my day. *Ciao, bella. Per me si va nella città dolente.* That's Dante."

"Mom, I know."

"They're teaching you Dante? I thought he went out with World War Two."

"I've read him myself. At school they're not teaching us anything except how to be stupid and popular."

"And find a girlfriend, no?"

"Oh. No, you don't get it. She's not my girlfriend. I don't think she is. I mean we're not, like, you know, doing anything. That's sort of what I wanted to ask you about. How do you tell?"

"How do you tell what?"

We've come to a fork in the road in the actual world. Left will take us to Morristown and right winds around placidly enough through truck farms and gardens that give this state its name. Though I've heard it called the armpit and worse. That's fine. Let it be our secret, we who live here. It's a good place for anyone who isn't poor and likes green. "Which way?" says Brighton.

"You decide. Left if you're hungry, right if you're starved for scenery."

"Did you bring any money?"

"Is the Pope Catholic?"

"Well, yeah. Of course he is. What do you mean?"

"Never mind, sweetie. It's just something people say."

"Oh. I get it. We say 'duh.' "

"Duh?"

"It means, that's obvious. You don't really say it to be nice. It's sort of negative."

"Duh."

"That's it, Mom." He laughs. "You've got it down. Let's go to the Ford News, okay? I'm sort of starving."

It's my favorite luncheonette, and his. They make an old-fashioned egg cream which means a lot to me, and a rare onion cheeseburger on a bulkie roll which means a lot to Brighton. We sit at a booth like we're on a date, though date for me always meant loss of appetite, and we're doing just fine in that department. He orders a second round for himself and I get a cup of hot tea, though at that moment, and always in this diner atmosphere, I wish I drank coffee. "How do you stay so skinny?" I ask him.

He shrugs. "I don't know. I'm not trying to."

"I think you've got a worm."

"I don't have a worm, Mom. A lot of kids are skinny. You were skinny I bet."

I'm thin now, and yes, I was skinny. Tall and slender to some, but in truth just skinny. I never wished it, though I was envied for it all through college. Biology is destiny, they say. I looked, and still do, slightly like Amelia Earhart.

I watch my son inhale his second hamburger. When he's done I'm his mother again, pointing out a ketchup smear on his cheek. It's still a soft cheek. I doubt he shaves yet. We're all late bloomers in this family. Tomorrow I turn forty and I feel like I'm still curled up fetal-like in my pod. Brighton reaches across the table and at first I'm certain he's come to take my hand, lead me somewhere, anywhere, out. But it's just my spoon he wants to borrow to sink a lemon slice down through the crushed ice glacier of his Coke.

"Mom," he says. "Can we finish talking about this stuff?"

"The girlfriend stuff?"

"Right. David says—"

"David?"

"Dr. Pearlman. He says we're sort of having, um, a relationship."

"Who is?"

"Me and Maria."

"You mean sleeping together?"

"Right. We're sort of doing that stuff without really knowing we're doing it. I think that sounds pretty weird, don't you?"

"Pretty weird."

"He says we have that energy for each other, we're just putting it in a different place. Like in music. She listens to these faggy groups with all this hair and not very clean and — "

"These faggy groups? You mean they're all homosexuals?"

He looks at me, shocked. Then he shakes his head quickly.

"I'm a stickler for language, okay? Be careful."

"Sorry."

"What else?"

"Nothing."

"You want me to say something? I can be your mom and say something."

"Go ahead."

"It's about this thing called sexual energy, which we all have. I think most of us have it most of the time, and who or what it goes to is basically irrelevant. Or haphazard. It doesn't much matter. It could go to this person or that, or this person one day and that one the next."

"Like a commune, Mom." He makes a face.

"Maybe like a commune, maybe not. We're human. We're not little sealed containers. Where it wants to go we send it. It can go right into your work. It can go to yourself. It doesn't have to mean sleeping with people. Wars are full of it. All conflict is. You have to connect with someone in order to argue with them, did you ever think of that?"

"Not really."

"To fight face to face you have to care about them. That's why in old wars they wore armor, to protect soldiers from their own compassion. And in new wars we fly way up and drop big bombs down where we can't see anything. Not grass huts, not villages, not human beings. We can barely see the ground. What would you do, how would you feel if you had to see the people you were about to kill, and they were all just doing what people do, carrying water, making food, feeding each other? Other things too. They were just like you. How would that feel?"

"Um, I don't know. Pretty bad. Mom?"

"It would feel pretty bad is right. We're deeply connected,

every one of us. If you show me someone I can't connect to, then you're leaving something out."

"But if you just care about someone, that doesn't mean it has to be, um, you know, sexual energy. If you're not, like, attracted to them."

"It's all the same to me. Energy. Call it whatever you want. The thing is you have to decide what to do with it. That's your human responsibility. Your adult human responsibility. You can listen to music, that's one way. Make love, that's another. Read books. Invent the wheel. Go out to lunch. Are you sick of this yet?" He nods, bless him. "I can't tell you if she's your girlfriend, Bright. If you like her and you decide you want to sleep with her and she decides she wants to sleep with you, well, I don't know what you want, my permission or your own. Without yours, mine won't mean a thing anyway. But don't be a dope, use birth control. Do you have things like that?"

"Mom, shut up," he says. "You're yelling."

Maybe I am. Anyway he has his head bowed. I've embarrassed him. Every time you turn a corner, you and your kid, there's a good chance one of you will die. We take turns dying, that's all I can hope. If one of us has to die more often I hope it's me. See, there it is again, I would step in front of a rushing train to save his life. Or at least to give away my own because of all I wish to escape, including the knowledge that I can't save him, not his life, not the pain of his growing and learning, not the scars already formed over the wounds already inflicted. Be careful, Tommie. This is a boy of glass in your stony hands. What did he do to deserve me?

Helen

When we were kids, my brother lived in a light reflected by me. He was a shade-loving plant, and the borrowed light of my goodwill and effort was enough to sustain him, though it did not make him shine. He did not want to shine. He wanted the earth to cover him. He wanted to wade in stony ground to his waist, hide his troublesome roots in clotty darkness.

I mean his sexuality. I mean his battle to contain himself in one part of his body — his head. He used me as his cover. I was there. I sheltered him. I took the attention he didn't want and digested it, like a mother bird, and fed it to him through the small, pink opening of his heart. It was surprising how I persisted, much of the time not knowing that I did so. The opening was almost imperceptible for many years. And when it started growing larger, during his time with Dr. Pearlman, he let others feed him — Maria, Tommie, even Dad and Hal. I lost my place and did not know it as my place until its absence.

He was kind to me, especially as he was leaving me behind. This was the hardest of all. He lost his rebel self and melted into an acquiescence I only briefly envied him for. He became good-natured and funny, and was obviously on his way to becoming handsome. Girls were drawn to him, girls who seemed an older version of me.

One night he came and sat on my bed and waited for me to look up from my homework. He never did homework. He just read books. He lived in books. He found his heroes there. He was always falling at the feet of someone else's invention. After a few minutes he said, "I can come back later, Helen." The bed wasn't made and I could feel his uneasiness as he sat there, his desire to tug my life into the kind of order he required. I let him sit. I kept my gaze on my math book, pretending a trance-like state of concentration. When he got up to go, I looked up and smiled at him feverishly.

"I'll come back," he said.

"No, I'm done."

"It can wait, really."

"I'm done, really." I slapped the book shut and dropped it on the floor. I pushed my chair out and turned to face him. "What's up?"

"I'm going to give you one of the chairs from my room. It's stupid you only have one chair."

"I only need one chair."

"Well, the other person has to sit on the bed."

"I'm not really worried about the other person."

He sat back down and said, "You don't have to answer this but I was wondering if you ever think, or, I don't know — yeah, think, about Faith." He looked at his knee and spoke to it. "You can say nothing if you want. That's okay."

"I never do," I said. "I never think about her."

"I used to."

"What's there to think about? There's nothing to think about. She wasn't even really a person."

"She was a person."

"She didn't even last one day."

He looked at me. I'd seen that look once before on the face of a much younger Brighton, the Brighton who fell through the ice and couldn't get himself back to us, whose effort dug him in deeper and whose only companion looked to be the unsolid ground which had betrayed him. He got up. I think he was wondering if I was really his sister. "Okay, Helen," he said, and bobbed his head in a curious way as if he were my servant. He stepped sideways out of the room, not willing to leave his back unguarded. That was the last of those visits.

Dad came in sometimes. It was easier to be with Dad than anyone else. He suddenly seemed like the only regular person I knew. If my light was on he'd come in after one of Hal's parties, before Mom got home. Waiting for her to come home was hard for him. He'd knock and poke his head in. I'd be in bed reading. "What are you doing up so late?" he'd say, but I could tell he was glad. "Want a Coke or something? I'm going to get myself a Coke." He brought our Cokes and held up his glass and looked at it and said, "I don't know why it took me so darn long to discover Coke."

"You want to sit, Dad?"

"No, I'll just stay a minute. I'll just stand. Boy, this room's a mess," he laughed, as one of my shirts wrapped itself around his ankle. He tried to shake it off, then leaned down and pulled it off and raised his finger and said, "Stay." He had a sense of humor. Nobody seemed to know that.

"I kind of like it messy."

He nodded. "It's your room. What happens in your room is your business."

"You don't really have a room."

"Well, I do. Your mother and I do."

"I wouldn't want to share a room with Mom. She's messier than me."

He smiled. "But I married her and you didn't. When you marry someone you expect to compromise. You want to compromise. You think it'll teach you something."

"Like what? Like being messy?"

"Well, like loosening up a little. It's funny. I didn't really like the Frank Haas who married your mother. He was a pretty dull guy. Predictable. A lousy dancer." He took a sip of his Coke. He looked out the window and shook his head. "She never fell in love with me, you know. I fell in love with her but she didn't fall in love back. Remember that, Helen. When you get to it, I mean. They ain't necessarily going to fall in love back."

"That's no good."

"No, but it's not bad. A marriage is a constant act of will. And faith. Your mother has a stronger will than I do, and almost no faith. I'm strong in both departments. Not when I met her. When I met her I had no will. See, she taught me that. After a while the falling in love doesn't matter. I don't know." He looked at me. "Maybe that's just what I like to think."

He was someone who showed himself in bursts, in the middle of the night, after a Coke or two, when the prospect of getting into bed without Tommie overwhelmed him. He was a series of small, bright explosions which most of the world slept through. I tried to be awake for him and usually I was.

One night at the beginning of June, I was in the shower and Brighton came in. He never came into the bathroom when I was in there, even if I was just brushing my teeth. This time he came in and stood in the steam while I finished my shower. I turned the water off and he said, "Don't hurry, Helen. There's nothing we can do." Then he told me another Kennedy had been shot.

That was right before Tommie's party. She had a big fortieth birthday party. After that nothing made sense to me for a long time. I spent a lot of time in my room. Sometimes I crossed the hall and went into Brighty's room if he wasn't there. I sat on his bed and looked at all his books. I looked on his dresser, at his comb and brush and hand lotion, and a little leather box he kept change in. I knew if I moved one thing on that dresser he'd know it. I knew I had no business going into his room and I couldn't even say why I did it except it was an okay way of not being Helen. I never went over to Hal's house anymore, even if Jody wasn't there. I couldn't handle Jody.

I had one friend at school, Brighty's friend Maria DiAngelo who was teaching me karate. Besides that I was alone all day long, going in and out of classrooms like some kind of lonely ship full of explosives that can't get permission to land anywhere. I felt like I was losing everything. I was losing my family, my friends, Hal. I was leaving my body behind too, my kid's body. It had been happening for a while but I hadn't noticed it or hadn't cared about it. I just never thought about it.

There were a lot of things I never thought about until Tommie turned forty. The country was a mess but I didn't notice. I was doing other things. You don't have that kind of vision when you're a kid. People love to impose their sense on things after the fact. You'd like to believe it, but if you lived through it you know it was just what it was, a mess you lived in like a messy room. You got used to it, the assassinations and riots and burnings and war and LSD and Haight-Ashbury and the Black Panthers and boys in your school going away and coming back in a casket. Not even them, pieces of them. You got used to it. It's called adaptation and it's good for the species. Like a whole generation suddenly looked down and discovered their opposable thumbs, discovered what they were good for after all these years, which was throwing bricks, throwing hand grenades and voting. Or shooting hoops if you were a kid like me. I played whatever sport was going, went home sweaty, ate like a horse and did my homework, then dropped into bed and slept. I never once thought about my life as my life, I just moved forward with the same sense of urgency that guides an animal.

Tommie's party involved a car accident that I was in. I broke my arm. It was my left arm and I'm right-handed. The cast went all the way up to my shoulder, the first cast did. There were three weeks left in the school year and I got a lot of attention for the cast and for my two black eyes, but it didn't sink in. It made it all worse. The only thing that sank in was something Maria said. I went up to her in the hall and told her, "Well, I guess that's it for the karate." Kids were going by us in a big hurry to get to the next class where they could just horse around and waste their lives. I always thought school should be optional. It doesn't do you any good if you just walk in with your body. That's what Maria said to me. First she said, "I'm sorry you broke your arm, Helen," and then she said we'd practice anyway if that was okay with me. We met in the gym and she said, "Go out and come back in again but this time don't bring in your body."

"Don't bring in my body? How do I do that?"

"Try it. Go back out and leave it out there."

I got the hang of it. We called it psychic karate. I got so that I could step out of my body whenever I wanted to. I still can. I can go far away, or hover, either one. Different situations call for different responses. When they took the cast off I hovered. My arm was a sick white, the same dirty white as the plaster, and sickly thin without muscles. But looking down on it from my perch I felt very peaceful and, I don't know, loving. You have to know when to leave and when to stay.

Something like this was already happening to me before the accident. I'd leave my body, but instead of hovering, I'd feel myself getting sucked into Tommie's body. Into her mind. I liked it at first. I didn't know what was happening. It was like watching a movie. It started with little things, like I knew when she was about to call upstairs to tell me lights out, or I knew when she would ask me to come in and change the channel on the TV. I always got a picture of the particular action in my mind. It would flash into my mind and then it would happen. "Sweetie, it's bedtime," would float up the stairs. It was fun. But if you've had this experience you know what happens next. You leave your seat in the theater and walk forward and melt into the screen, into the movie itself. You can't help it. A friend of mine who used to do a lot of drugs says this is the point where a trip becomes a bad trip if you let it. I don't know what that means, "if you let it." For me it was never an option. I had premonitions about Tommie. The night of the accident I knew what was coming to her. After that I couldn't get far enough away from her, and I still knew.

Tommie

I did not abandon them, I left them. I left them and went to Pennsylvania for a while, then out to the west coast where I knew no one and no one, thank God, knew me. I had no intention of never coming back, and I did come back. I took a leave of absence for the summer and now I'm lodged again in my old home.

I hate it. I've made some changes to like it more but they seem petty and embarrassing. Frank said, What is it? What can we do? What can we change? How can I keep you is what he meant. I said put a mirror in the bedroom. In the bedroom? On the ceiling. Over the bed. I want to watch myself at every turn because I don't trust what I can't see. Now it haunts me. To look up and see his pale backside toiling. What was I thinking? It was a dare. I feel like a middle-aged woman here and all summer I felt like rain. Like rain in sudden places. I felt my skin flame up and steam. I'm not an idiot. Jeanne Ann has as little to do with it, she personally, as Frank does. It comes from Tommie, it's Tommie's weather. Cumulus with anvil. Nimbus with fork and spoon. Thunder head, lightning body. I miss it. I miss that way of me that loves until it falls.

Jeanne Ann says I have webbed hands, a larger-than-usual pouch between fingers. These are the endearments of two old women. We used to say I like you, you smell nice, I like the way you look, your hair is beautiful, your ass is glory. Now it's the extra skin we notice and love. Or don't love. Her body is still as fit as a tree, mine hangs on me like an apron. Not fat. Limp. Like the feast of my life left no impression as it passed through me. Or passed me by.

Frank's crowd, his business acquaintances (like me, the man has no friends), caught wind of something afoot in our home. No morning and evening wife at the station, none of Tommie's pot roast under his belt. Mussed shirts until Brighton took over the ironing. The boy's a natural. Mr. Fastidious. I watch him now, watch him enter his trance at the ironing board. He's like a machine with feelings. Feed him shirts, slightly damp, and he's happy. He rocks. He's hearing music I don't hear. That's the trick with children. Let them rock on their own two feet and love the chores we hate. It was good for them, their summer without me, wasn't it? Frank learned to lie, Brighton learned to iron, and Helen learned to hate me openly. There's a fault between us now, fault as in chasm, across which man and boy lay their little bridges, their little Band-Aids. All summer long on the phone it was Brighton: "Hi, Mom, how are you? How's California? How's the ocean?" Frank: "We're fine here. How's your money holding up?" Not Helen. Helen my athlete-warrior, my shadow, goes the other way, all entrenched. We are like each other in that movement. Remote as ever. Seeking the truth. Lonely. Brave. When I left she was the only one who had nothing to say. The others treated me like an illness, like an ill woman in an unstable state of mind on the verge of a disastrous mistake for which she is not responsible. Frank still does not hold me responsible, he lays that honor on Jeanne Ann.

It was not a complicated departure. I packed a suitcase, said good-bye and drove away in my car. No Rapunzels, no bedsheet ropes, no hunchbacks, no promises. Since my party I'd taken to sleeping on the downstairs couch with my clothes on. Maybe I felt soiled, maybe I felt punishable, maybe I anticipated my husband's forgiveness and it made me too angry, too humiliated to sleep. I'd had nothing to drink for two weeks, doctor's orders, post-concussion precautions having to do with the fact that I'd seized mildly the day after the party and they were "monitoring," oh monitoring, those serious professionals. Crack the windshield with your own skull and you'd go epileptic too, gentlemen. We totaled a car. Never mind. My head swam constantly, even in my dreams which were few. They were frightening things, full of sexual distortions. Me going at it with a loaf of bread while my children, all three of them, watched with glee. Night sweats, calling out, my own voice waking me from what could be called sleep. It was gin deprivation. Better no sleep than this. I had a drink in the dark, sitting up in the dark on my bed of nails, facing away from the open window which promised cool freedom, looking instead at the stairs that led up to my sleeping, dreaming family. I had no doubt I loved them, a burning clarity. I knew just how they slept: Frank sprawled, flung wide as he never was in his waking life; Helen in a long tight line on her back; Brighton face down without a pillow. Frank and Helen in pajamas, Brighton in his underwear.

We're a family that dribbles down to eat when we feel like it on weekends. I set the table and brought out boxes of this and that, dry cereals, milk, English muffins. The comfort of familiar foods was my thought. I made coffee and tea and hot chocolate and waited for them. Frank first, Brighton, Helen. I said, "I'm going away for a while. Maybe a week, maybe more. I'm going to stay with Jeanne Ann. I'll take my car. That leaves you the new one, cha cha cha. Her number's by the telephone." Or something like that. As I say, Helen was the only one with any sense. She went upstairs to her room without a word. The other two fussed, the little whiny protests of children who need naps.

"Tommie, you can't," said Frank.

"Can't?"

"With a head injury. You're crazy to drive."

"But not crazy to go."

"No, you're crazy to go, too. You're upset. Of course you are. I understand that. But to go running off someplace where there's no medical help if you need it, no routine to fall back on, no family, no friends."

"That's exactly what she is."

"Well, I don't get it. Who knows what shape she's in. It's a crazy thing to do. Wait a week. Why don't we make a plan. Plan for it. Go in a week if you still feel like it."

"Does she know you're coming, Mom?"

"I'll call her from the road."

"Why don't you call her now? That way she'll be expecting you. If she's not expecting you, she may not be there, and if she's not there the house is maybe locked."

"Thank you, Brighton. You make it kindergarten clear, but I'll call her from the road."

"Boy, are you in some kind of mood."

"It will improve, I assure you."

"There are certain logistics," said Frank. "One, how will we deal with getting these two to wherever they need to go, and me to the station? One car's going to make it tough, Tommie."

"Then rent one. Borrow one of Hal's. Use your imagination. Ask your son to drive you to the train. Carpool. Call on your friends, see what they're made of. Take a cab. Come on, Frank. Let go."

As I drove away I thought of Hal. I couldn't see it, but I knew just where it was, that brown spot on the lawn where the tent had been and our dancing feet had killed the grass. Brighton would tell him I'd left. Once it had been Helen but now it was Brighton. Curious. When had that love affair cooled and why? I felt a surge of loyalty to my own and knew that if he'd been careless, if Hal had, I'd kill him. Turn the mirror on yourself, Tommie.

I stayed with Jeanne Ann from the middle of June until the end of July. Her face wasn't disfigured, but she had a nasty, Frankenstein-like cut on her forehead at her hairline, and both arms were covered with small wounds. The windshield I shattered with my head had landed like a phoenix in her lap. Helen said it rained glass.

She lives outside of Pittsburgh in a small town that will, in ten years, have lost its character and become a suburb. I'm not much of a one for flora and fauna, but I remember her pointing to some sort of unremarkable tree and saying, the ubiquitous horse chestnut. As for the rest, there was sky like anywhere else and heat that discouraged anything, any movement but slippery love. Green grass, green everywhere, green, green, green. We were drowning in it. Storms came regularly, thunder, epileptic lightning.

It was not the same as being college roommates. It wasn't the same as almost being lovers in my house with Brighton in diapers and Helen in utero and Frank always, and possibly thankfully, in the way. Big talker, Tommie. Big, big, talker. This was just me and Jeanne Ann, ourselves. She doesn't even own a television. She has a window onto her yard, and another window which looks into a dense, woody place full of what I call pine trees but which are actually not. Pine does not equal evergreen. That's how scientists speak. Anyway, that window made me happy. I liked the sudden leap to darkness and greenness. I didn't need to explore it, I needed to look at it. I felt starved for darkness. I needed great swatches of darkness to feed on. Ever since my children were born I'd aimed so hard at the light, the happy, the up. A positive attitude. It just wasn't natural to me. Of course it didn't work. The whole project was a dismal failure. I'm sure if they remember me for anything it will be for my bite. My bitter root as Hal calls it. Well, goddamn the effort.

One day I said to her, "Come here." I pointed out the window. "What does that say to you?"

"What?"

I laughed. "There's no right answer, Jeannie." I'd taken to calling her Jeannie, like Hal did.

She sat down on the arm of the chair. "What does what say?"

"You know. The trees. The way they are. The way they stop right there and then there's the space and then there's us."

"I think you're happy, Tommie. That's what it says."

She got up and left and it was the first time in a long time I'd felt hungry for someone. Desire, I thought, oh, I recognize you. Welcome.

She teaches chemistry at the University of Pittsburgh and most of her friends are women, and many of them are lesbians. She had a party for me one Sunday afternoon. People came and cooked drippy things on a grill and drank beer and ate carrot sticks. They had short, fierce haircuts and fat arms and droopy breasts and fat thighs barely covered by mannish looking shorts. No thank you. Afterwards I said to Jeanne Ann, "I don't understand why women do that to themselves." I was sitting in the kitchen watching her put things away. She's orderly, slow, thoughtful, and I'm not. Just then it annoyed me.

"Do what to themselves?"

"Stuff their fat bodies into ugly clothes that make them look like men. Are they trying to be men? I don't get it."

"Of course you don't get it. You wouldn't. How could you?"

"Meaning?"

"Oh, wake up, Tommie. You're a married woman and you'll stay that way by choice. This is just a game for you, this loving. But you like it. Boy, do you like it. So you better find something to stand in the way of what comes next, and big women, big braless women relaxing together with their loved ones on a Sunday, they're an easy target."

"What comes next? Sleeping with strangers? Fucking everyone in sight?"

"I wish you could hear yourself. Mrs. Frank Haas."

"That woman Pat kept putting her hand on me."

"You're attractive. Why wouldn't she? She's a single woman and she liked you, she was being friendly. You put your hand on me all the time, what's the difference?"

"I know you. I don't know her."

"I think you're discovering something." She turned around, ketchup bottle in one hand, dishcloth in another. It infuriated me, a twentieth-century woman wiping a bottle.

"What am I discovering? Tell me, O Great One."

She snorted. "Go away, Tommie. You're mining us. We're not yours to use up and throw away."

"Ah, the old cliché."

"Get out of here."

I was evicted. I got in the car and drove straight through to Washington State, stopping only for gas and naps. There was no reason to go there or anywhere. The scenery was insignificant, the food was bland. I don't like mountains. I picked up a young hitchhiker somewhere, a boy, a Brighton, and left him off somewhere else as the sun was going down outside a low, wet building with a sign that said *Meals*. The rain was ceaseless. I thought of everything and came to no conclusions. I was alone. I went down through Oregon and into California, amazed at the brown cloth of summer on those hills, and the stillness of the valleys with their red crops. I felt lazy-sexual in the heat. I wondered if the boy, the hitchhiker, had expected me to make love to him. It was a long, vague trip. I was only its passenger.

You tell the story you can. Of course I'm struggling with who I am in bed. I'm not ashamed, but frightened by a woman's love. Before this summer that wasn't the case. I've left out great chunks, all the fleshy parts with Jeanne Ann, where before I would have said them first. They became more sacred. I became more scared. Listen. This is Tommie talking.

You know now that she came to my party and at the end of the evening we cracked up a car. Helen was with us. She broke her left arm. She couldn't shoot baskets against the garage and she couldn't swim. These were her expressed woes, the others went passive aggressive. I was drunk. I'm told I was drunk though I don't remember, which isn't the evidence it seems. This wasn't a booze blackout. The doctors call it a "window." It's a period of amnesia due to a head injury. I have a window of about four to six hours. I remember putting on Frank's birthday present — maybe it was a joke but I wore it anyway — a paper dress. What do I care? Mrs. Living Garbage Bag. I had on some flat shoes and sat demurely in my husband's car waiting to be chauffeured by him to the Chapin estate across the fence. Not fence, field. May we never need a fence, neighbor. It was raining lightly. I hung my arm out the window as we drove down our driveway and up Hal's. Helen and Brighton were over there already, setting up, whatever that meant. I noticed my son was wearing one of Hal's bow ties. Helen couldn't believe my costume, in fact groaned. Hal took one look and laughed, he in a peaches and cream suit, light gray shirt and off-white bow tie and bucks. I don't know what the boyfriend wore. Something black and tan. Helen said, "Gross, Tommie. It's puffing up in the rain." And it was. Clothing as enemy. My gown turning to pulp and making me look fat as a potato.

I remember the obscene color and dimensions of the tent — a bilious mushroom under which we wee folk ate and danced. I remember dancing with Hal who can dance and Frank who cannot. We were polite to each other that evening, my husband and I. He can't help it. I can. Brighton came up to me. Would I like to meet his girl? Sure. He didn't say "girl," he said "friend." She was big, bigger than my son. Not tall. Big-boned. Substantial. She was a woman, dressed in black with breasts that pressed against the front of her blouse, hips to cradle babies. She was attractive in a Sicilian way and not at all Brighton's type. I'm not jealous, I'm all-knowing. I offered my hand. "Have you ever met anyone so old?" I said. "I'm practically dead."

"Mom," said Brighton, looking away.

"Don't worry," she said, "I've got a couple of dead ones at home."

"Her parents are really old," he said.

She laughed. "Sixty."

She and Helen danced. "Not you, Bright?" I asked.

"No. I'm not really a good dancer."

"They must know each other. They act like it."

"She's teaching Helen karate."

"Is that what we're watching?"

"I think they're just dancing, Mom."

My serious son. "Go fill up your hollow leg and bring me something," I said. "Something wicked."

"You mean like those Chinese meatballs?"

"Wicked, Brighton. Cheesy, puffy, fattening. At least. And some pâté. If there's black caviar I want that too. Frogs' legs," I called after him. "Don't croak."

He turned and grinned at me. "Mom, you're a trip."

Hal appeared and I asked him, "What does that mean, 'Mom, you're a trip'?"

"I think it's thumbs up." He nodded at the dance floor. "Now there's a couple."

"She's Brighton's girl."

"Dressed for a funeral?"

"Don't be funny, I already had that thought. She's not his type, is she?"

"No."

"Why do you hesitate?"

"I don't hesitate. She's not his type."

"Something's going through your head."

"At all times, let's hope."

"Hal? It's not right for you to fall in love with my children, you know that? It's all right for you to fall in love with them but not really. You know that."

"To fall in love with them but not really."

"A long, fruitless courtship, all right?"

He laughed.

"It's not a joke, Hal."

He put his arm through mine. "Your friend is here," he said.

"They're your friends and I see them all. They were brave to come."

"Tommie." He took my hand and led me out into the rain.

We walked across the driveway, into the field of parked cars. Except for the rain it was just the time when a man would lead a woman outside to kiss her and fondle her breasts. Dusk. I hoped he would, suddenly. He led me down the second row, all the way to the end near the foot of the driveway. "So many cars," I said.

"Uh huh."

"What are we doing, Hal?"

"Paying a visit."

I heard the soft noise of a radio coming from the last car, a little Volkswagen. Its windows were open, letting the rain in. We passed in front of it and Hal knocked lightly on the hood and she got out. "Package for you," he said to her. "You're not leaving tonight, Jeannie?"

"No. I'll stay somewhere."

"Well, stay with me if she won't have you. You know I'm fun." He kissed her, then he kissed me. "I've got to go play hostess. See you."

Tommie at a loss for words for once. Finally I said, "Well, he's proud of himself. So he knew you were coming?"

"No. No one knew. I didn't know. What is this, Tommie? What have you got on?"

"Frank gave it to me. It's a dress."

"It looks like a pastry."

"I'm not really this fat. I think the rain ruins it."

"Something does. What's it made of?" She felt it. "It's slimy. It feels like flour and water. We could bake you."

"It's paper."

She laughed. "Get in. Get in and roll up the window. That's better."

We were stuck then. A parked car often gives the illusion of velocity; at least in my life this has been the case. But we went nowhere. I believe there was nowhere we wanted to go. Ahead of us was my house. We sat looking forward with our hands in place, hers on the wheel, mine in my lap. Then we both spoke at once. She said, "How are your kids?" and I said, "I don't think I know what I want."

"What?"

"I don't think I know what I want."

"Why should you? You're only forty." She brought my hand to her lap. "How are your kids?"

"They seem to exist without me."

"You're feeling tragic tonight."

I turned my face to her. "I'm happy to see you."

"Well, ditto."

"I hate it when you say that."

She hadn't changed much in her body. Funny how these things are still important, how our radar flies to this one and not that one. Chemistry. Well, she was the teacher. I hadn't seen her for a couple of years, maybe three years, when we passed a joint back and forth in Hal's living room. It was my first time, those two had done it before. I didn't like it. I got too high too fast, but not floaty like booze. I felt like I'd swallowed metal. Jeanne Ann massaged me, that helped. We never talked about the scene in the bathtub. Were we waiting to? I don't know. I don't always believe in talk.

"I think I'm going to get myself a drink," I said.

"I'm not ready for a party, Tommie."

"I'm not either, but that's where the booze is. I'll get us both a drink and come back."

This is where the window begins to close. I search my brain and don't remember. Hal tells me we walked in out of the rain together. Jeanne Ann said her helloes to my husband and children. The only other one she knew was Bobby Kahn — and Erica, Hal's ex, who was held up somewhere but on the way. She and Bobby danced. She and I did not. Why not? How stupidly unlike you, Tommie. I can do what I want, it's my party. Around midnight the pool began to be popular. Brighton's friend Maria threw him in. Bobby the bachelor and Jeanne Ann took a plunge. "Undressed?" I asked Hal.

"Bobby was."

"How did Brighton do? He hates the water."

"He thrashed around until the young Aida rescued him. She dragged him out. He wouldn't speak to her. I think they'll be good friends someday. Like us."

"Where was Helen?"

"Your shadow?"

"My shadow?"

"That's why she got in the car with you, Tommie. She never let you out of her sight after you and Jeannie came in. She dogged you. I watched her. She wasn't herself. She knew something. I think she had a premonition."

"Oh, come on."

"She looked blank in the face, like she'd left her body."

"She was probably high."

She and the young Aida was my thought. Who knows what that one carried in under her black blouse, besides what she was born with. Helen in search of a role model turns to a life of crime. Well, better that than follow me. But strange that she should hang on my coattails all night long when she could have hung on Maria's. My pulpy coattails. It occurred to me I knew nothing about drugs, didn't know what was what, didn't know who to ask, was afraid to find out. They both seemed so wholesome, those girls. They were athletes, they worshipped their bodies. Maybe Helen had a desperate edge these days but I took it for a passing, existential thing, a tapping into Who Am I? In school she was reading *The Stranger,* of course. *Pippi Longstocking* one year, *The Stranger* the next. Schools steal our children if you ask me. No one should read *The Stranger.* I don't believe in books. I don't believe in anything I didn't write myself. Read nothing until the age of gullibility is past. I lost my son to books.

Hal has described the accident, has reconstructed events to fill the window. Everyone has their version of the story. I feel like an island where tourists come to walk the ruins which are nothing much, and feeling cheated they fill their pockets with pieces of the old wall. Just to have something. Having is so important to us. Who would we be if we didn't have? If he's right — and he isn't of course, any more than bones describe a life (partial truth) — we got in the car, Frank's car, Jeanne Ann, Helen and I to meet a train with Erica on it, and ran into bad luck on the way. Had it been on the way back, Erica or Helen would have died, and probably Helen. Sometime in the wee hours Erica called from a Morristown motel room and said a wounded, well-you've-forgotten-about-me goodnight. "Where are you?" said Hal. She named the place and he said, "Isn't Tommie with you?"

"Nobody is with me. I am here alone. I waited for a long time in the station and when nobody came I gave up on you. Now I have rented a bed." Icelandic for found a motel.

"Tommie's not with you?"

"Hal. I am not blind. I am tired and I will come over to say my regards in the morning. Now I would like just to sleep."

Hal went upstairs and woke up Jody. There were bodies all over the living room, limp, inebriated, but at least warm to the touch. And he did, he said he did, he walked through the room and touched all of them. It was one of those things people do in the teeth of a crisis, slow to a snail's pace and find importance in the small. He called up Frank who had gone off to bed around midnight when people began to loosen up and have fun. "Christ," said Frank, "what time is it?" Hal could hear him rubbing his face.

"Almost three."

"Let me get my bearings here. Okay. Here I am. Hey, that was some party. It really was. Thank you."

He went on a little and Hal let him. This was Frank at his ingenuous best, waking up in the middle of the night without me, reaching for his glass of water. Finally he said, "Did you call me or did I call you?"

"I called you."

"That's what I thought. Is she in a heap somewhere? Do you want me to come get her?"

"I'm not sure where she is, Frank."

"Oh. Wait a minute." Incredibly, he searched the bed. My name was called. "Not here either. She hasn't been here."

"I think she's between here and Morristown. She's in your car, she took your car, she and Helen and Jeanne Ann."

"Why did she take my car? She's got her car. She probably took her car. What do you mean? Where did they go?"

He was awake now, he was getting the gist of it. This made it harder for him but easier for Hal. Hal explained what he knew, that Erica caught a late train out, the red-eye, and I volunteered to pick her up. Jeanne Ann and Helen went along for the ride. The train was due in around one o'clock. We never arrived.

"What the Christ is Helen doing up?" He was pulling on some clothes at the same time. "Wait. I'll be right over." He met

Hal and Jody in their driveway a couple of minutes later. I don't know this for a fact but I can guess that on his way out he looked in on his sleeping son.

He sat next to Hal, who drove. Jody sat in the back. Frank said, "She was driving? Who was driving?"

"I don't know," said Hal.

"Why did they go all the way to Morristown?"

"I don't know where they went. I don't know how far they got."

"Why didn't they pick her up here? That's my question."

"The train doesn't stop here."

"What do you mean it doesn't stop here?"

Jody said, "It doesn't make local stops, Frankie, not in the middle of the night." Frank absorbed the Frankie and said nothing. "I know because I used to take it all the time, chasing this guy." He leaned forward and started to rub Hal's shoulder. "Anyone else got the feeling they're in a ditch somewhere?"

Hal shrugged him off. "I can't drive when you do that."

"You need a little massage. Your neck's so tight. It's like a rope."

"I can't do two things at once right now."

"You don't have to. Just drive, I'll massage you. These kinds of situations make people very tense, it's good to have some-body working on you. Relax."

"I can't relax. Not with you doing that."

"Try."

"For Christ's sake," said Frank, "will you leave him alone? The man's driving."

"Jesus," said Jody. He slumped back against the seat. "What are we looking for, anyway? What kind of car?"

"A green Volvo," said Frank. "A dark green sedan."

"You know the car, Jody. It's Frank's car."

"I guess I know it. I didn't know it was dark green. It's an old one, isn't it?"

The rain had stopped but there were deep puddles in the road. "It must have really rained here," said Hal.

"It looks slippery as shit," said Jody. "I don't get why you people don't put shoulders on your roads, or guardrails or something. You have an accident, a little sideswipe, and the car rolls over into a ditch and people end up getting hurt, for nothing."

Frank shook his head. He was straining to see through the dark, right into the future. I can see him, poor man. His jaw is set, his politeness is eroding. Much longer and he'll kill the mouth in the back seat. He's suddenly not afraid of life. He's angry. "What did she think she was doing?" he said. He turned to Hal. "What the hell did she think she was doing?"

"It sounded tame enough," said Hal. "It was her night, her party, she wanted to pick up Erica so she went. You know Tommie."

"I don't mean Tommie. Helen."

"Right dead ahead of you," said Jody.

"I see it," said Hal.

Not the Volvo, but the implications of it. A cluster of flashing red and blue activity which meant cops and ambulance. A hundred yards away he slowed to a crawl. No reason, except not wanting to get there, not wanting to know. Frank wanted to know and he pointed at the wheel. "Drive," he said hoarsely, "or I will."

"What a mess," said Jody.

"You hear that?" said Frank. "I hear them."

"That's a bullhorn," said Jody. "It's a cop on a bullhorn."

"Listen."

They listened. It was Helen. She was calling someone a fucking ape. "You hairy fucking ape, you dick shit, you motherfucking dick shit pig. Let go of me." That's an approximate litany. A cop tried to wave them around but Hal pulled over and stopped, headlights on. Frank was already out and running into the flashing lights. He almost ran into the Volvo, saw it was empty and started to kick it, crying, clawing his face. "Helen! Helen, where are you? It's Dad." Blinded by the flashers, he threw an arm up over his eyes. "Where are you, sweetie? I'm here. Sweetheart, I'm here. Daddy's here."

So says Hal. Frank doesn't tell this story and Helen has never said a word to me about anything that happened that night. To her brother, yes, to her father, but never to me. I don't expect it. Her life was becoming different and that night was the blow that struck home. All the other blows struck somewhere, the unsung heroes, the unknown soldiers of a kid's need to grow up and go away, but that one hit a place any idiot could look at and point to and say, it was never the same after this. This is where it began.

She broke her arm in two places, above and below the elbow. It was a terrible break. The radius came right through the skin. Something obscene about that, the intimate bone crying to the surface, virgin white against the pink flesh and gore. I didn't see it, thank God. I was nowhere by then. I was in my room behind blackout curtains waiting for the war to begin. In other words, unconscious. Jeanne Ann was in and out of consciousness — shock and a deep head wound. She saw things, visions. When the windshield fell on her she saw a woman putting on a glass dress. Much later she was aware of Helen moving her out of the driver's seat.

Helen was driving when the police found us. She was driving on three rims and without headlights along the narrow shoulder of the road. The Volvo looked like a bomb hit it but she was steering confidently, one-armed, going in the only gear she could find. She told the cop she was going home. She was hard to stop. She didn't want to stop for anyone for the same reason Hal, a hundred yards from us, didn't want to go forward. She thought I was dead and she wanted to keep that between us, our secret. If she could contain it she could keep going, and if she could keep going long enough what was true would change. I felt that way about Faith. When they told me her heart had stopped I waited for Frank to come, and when he came I didn't tell him. We talked about the hospital food, the snow, the rain, I don't know. The minute I told him was the minute she died.

Helen escaped death that night by sitting where she could watch me, behind Jeanne Ann who was driving. Her usual seat was directly behind the passenger. There was nothing left of that part of the car when we were done. Jeanne Ann says it was like being in a car with a magnet, that she, Helen, was utterly still and never took her eyes off me.

"Why? Was there something to watch? If there was something, I want to know it."

"There was nothing, Tommie."

"Was I touching you? Did I say something?"

"No, nothing. We were just driving. Helen was burning a hole in the side of your head for her own reasons. You're not guilty. There was nothing we did to invite what happened. The road was slick and it went out from under me, that's all. Bobby had some terrific pot and that didn't help, but after the swim, getting in the car I felt fine. It was an accident, a mistake."

"I don't believe in accidents, and I hate mistakes."

"Poor you. The wheel was invented by mistake."

"Screw the wheel," I said.

On one of the bad corners on the road to Morristown the car did a one-eighty, slid across the road and slammed sideways into a stone wall. I know that road and it's the only stone wall on it.

We use fences in New Jersey. That wall came down from Connecticut just to meet us. The Volvo people offered Frank a lot of money to photograph the car for an advertisement for the company. "This car drove away from it," or some such thing. He refused, though it would have paid some bills around here. Helen's on her third cast, unsigned I notice, but the other two were hardly a packed house either. I wonder who she is in her little world.

I finally asked her if she'd ever done drugs — I think "done" is the word I used. Hip but not too hip, that was my path to walk, I decided. We were left alone in the same room together for more than ten seconds, and before she bolted I dropped the question. I won't say she'd have passed a lie detector test with the look she gave me. She collapsed around the mouth, something I personally distrust. Followed by a not-too-convincing "Mom, are you crazy?" But at least it was out in the open. I'd done something to let her know she wasn't invisible at all times, that what she did mattered.

We don't have conversations. We do have encounters. For example, in a moment of generosity she tells me this: "If my door is shut, I don't want you coming in."

"Fine. If it's shut, it's shut, Helen. I don't go into your room anyway."

"Yes, you do."

"Excuse me, but I don't."

"You were in there yesterday, Tommie."

What does she do, track me? Or is it the trick with the hair across the crack of the door? She's right. I'd forgotten. I went in to close her window after she left for school. That side of the house gets hit hardest with rain. "The mistake is mine," I said. "From now on close your own window."

"I like it open. I don't care if it rains in."

Now we're down to the destruction of property, and whose property is it? "I care," I said. "It's not a way to treat a house."

"It's not your house, it's all of ours."

"You ruin the windowsill and someone has to come in and replace it and that someone has to be paid."

"I'll pay them. You don't pay them anyway, Tommie. Dad does."

You see who we are? We are the fifteen-year-old and her mother. We are the locked horns, the mirror turned on each other, and each other's blind spot. We are old love gone down into the earth to die. With any luck a seasonal death. How long is a season? The world shrinks as we get older, becomes a smaller place to make mistakes in.

Helen explained my summer absence with an irony that made me laugh. She told her friends, anyone who asked (the curious minions), that her mother went away to have an abortion. She handed me a limelight when I just as easily could have been visiting relatives, a sick aunt. Or looking for a dog to buy, an animal of stature — that was one of Frank's incredible lies. Brighton is quiet on the subject. I think he actually doesn't care who I am or what I do, though he'd like me to be happy. What a kid. I'd like you to be Donald Duck, Mom. That's just as likely.

Before the summer he finished up with Dr. Pearlman. Relief to me, it padded the wallet again, but this fall I thought he might need to go back and I offered him that. "It's been a strange summer in this little family," I said. "He knows you. He's someone you can talk to."

"I like David," he said, "but we're, you know, not social friends or anything. Did you mean pay him?"

"I did."

"Forget it, Mom. There's other people I can talk to, don't worry."

And there are, I notice. It's obvious. Where have I been? There's Hal. Brighton spends evenings over there with Hal and Jody, watching television or playing Scrabble. The rest of his friends are woodsy girls. They come as a unit. Maria's one of them. They do things in the forest under full moons and I don't ask what. Frank asks what. He doesn't ask Brighton, he asks me. In bed. "What do you think they're up to out there?"

"I have no idea. Go to sleep."

"Whatever it is, it's on our property."

"If you're going to worry out loud, go find out."

He ignores this. "Is he the only male? The rest are girls?"

"I know as little about it as you do."

"They're not stargazing, Tommie."

"No. They're not playing Scrabble either."

"I think we're responsible for them. What do you think?"

I don't know what I think. I think it's a hard question.

Frank gets up. He goes to the window that faces the wooded hill behind our house. He's in his pajamas. I never wear anything to bed and I buy him flannel pajamas that feel good against my skin. I'd buy him silk but he wouldn't wear them. Hal wears silk pajamas.

"They've got a fire going," he says. I get up and stand next to him and I can see it too, the orange stripes between the trees. It's a big fire, tall, like a shock of hair. "Do you think they know what they're doing?" he says, and puts his arm around my naked waist. "You're cold, Tommie."

We watch for a while, my right side warmed by the flannel and my left side longing to join the fire, join that circle of female energy generous enough to include my son. I have a feeling they're making a decent lover out of him, that's what these sessions are about. I imagine him under their hands, his teachers, his long body newly his and a miracle to him after years of reading alone in his room. Is it indecent to imagine your own child feeling his way through the infant stages of sex with another human being? I'm a mother, and I'm willing him all that I don't have.

Frank nudges me towards the bed and I let him, passive, knowing he'll want to make love to me now. My skin still responds to him, which makes life easier for both of us. He's steady and predictable, always courteous about orgasm, my orgasm. I live in a shallow sexual world with him, but for the moment, it's our world.

As soon as I feel him drop off to sleep I think about the day. He lets go in sleep the way he does inside me, with the same muscle spasms, the last resistance, the last softening. The little death, as the French call orgasm, with their need to reduce all acts of the body to poetry. *Grand mal. Petit mal.* The little illness. I wonder if mine are little or grand.

I had another one today, another seizure. It came as they all do in the wake of a powerful need to make love. I've told no one. They are my secret, a secret life for Tommie, like having the lover I don't have, a daytime lover while Frank's at work and the kids are at school. They come between nine and eleven in the morning. I wait for them. I fear them. There's an excitement in my body that translates into sexual energy that translates into seizure. There isn't a color or shape to the aura. None of the senses. Some people taste metal or smell burning rubber or hear Beethoven or dogs barking. There is only the sensation of deep sexual longing.

This is the fourth one. After the first there was nothing all summer until I came home. That was five weeks ago. They only happen in this house and only when I'm alone. They aren't unpleasant. I wake up on the floor and remember nothing. They leave me softened and weepy and with a headache and dizziness for the rest of the day. To my family I become someone slightly nostalgic and daft, like a deaf uncle.

Sometimes I think I'll tell Hal but he's not to be trusted. He'd fuss. I don't want to be fussed over. I want to be left alone but cared for. I want to feel wanted but not necessary, not vital. It's a symbolic act, but I turn to the man next to me and say his name. "Frank?" It's not designed to wake him. I know this man. When he sleeps he sleeps. "I'm going away again. Not soon, but someday. I'm going away to live with my own people. There are worse afflictions."

Frank

I don't know how it is for other men, but when I first saw my wife I wanted to be her. She wasn't my wife then, she was a girl at a dance. Every time I looked at her, "Some Enchanted Evening" ran through my head. The crowded room, the stranger; and so in the end I asked her to foxtrot with me. I must have been crazy. If so, it was the first time in my life.

My feet are large and I occupy them thoughtlessly, as if they are another country and I an eager visitor without a guidebook. I left Tommie with two bruised insteps and someone to laugh at, I'm afraid.

I wanted to be her. I wanted to be as self-assured as she appeared, and as at home in her — I don't know what to call it but her body. Though it was not quite her body. It was not just her body. Ease seemed to rise from her skin and permeate the skin of her neighbor, whoever he might be. For one brief dance it was me. I could feel it come and I could feel it go. Its going was a complete surprise to me because for some reason related to youth, and possibly to *South Pacific,* I had assumed once we touched hands I would never be without her.

It isn't a bad idea to get all the disappointments over with at the beginning. Ease was never the essence of my wife, though early on she suggested it strongly. She was a girl full of kick and life and hard, unbending opinions, some of them about me. I was a polite, decent, slightly dull fellow without a teasing bone in my body, completely unprepared for the firestorm that was Tommie.

In my mind I call her Margaret. She was christened Margaret. I want her to be Margaret, my tame, old-fashioned wife. She sits by me in the evenings and darns my socks. We talk of my work, our interests, our children, our disappearing life. We make small jokes that are funny to us and to no one else because they are lived, not invented. We have our years together, Margaret and I. Sometimes I think to myself, well then, who is this Tommie? And the answer comes to me: she saves you from yourself, Frank Haas. Your dull, dry self might have died with Margaret. Your cautious self. Tommie is your chaos and your sleepless years of worry; she is your ship, and she is your wife; she is Helen's mother, and Brighton's, and she held your daughter Faith before she died and did not tell you of that death as you came in the room because she is now and was then the only one who knew how hard you would fall. You stood beside her bed, remember? feeling little Faith's promise. Snow in November. One hell of a ride back to the hospital. My wife in the bed. Her hair a messy knot on the pillow, a nest we would later have to cut out, like cutting out the heart of an animal, which by then had been done to us we both felt. Tommie's brave chitchat until she saw I was braced against her and ready. Her tears the size of marbles. Mine which never came. Two people hope to win something together, but more often they lose and forget that to lose together is as powerful as to win.

One thing I have learned from my living children is the liability of a good imagination. I did not begin to know my children until they themselves shook me out of my dream. My wife brought an ax to that dream over and over again, countless times in our marriage, and yet in my mind it cleaved molecules of dust.

I did not often tend to Brighton and Helen. They were in their mother's care by day, and at night they were in bed. Helen and I sometimes read the paper together as she got older. I was an absent family man. I exerted no effort and took all for granted. I may never have washed a dish in the first nineteen years of my marriage, and I know I never cooked, not even an egg, not even a steak on the grill. I earned the money to make those steaks possible, but I could not do more than that. I was a dead man on weekends.

So it took a great shock, a visual display of what appeared to be fireworks — red, white and blue — to shake me out of my old complacency and into the life of the family. Even the word family was a new discovery for me. It had always meant duty and perseverance and swallowing one's pride, and making more money. It had never had a living quality to me, not since the day — the hours of the day — Faith lived and died. She stunned me. The little creature I met once, touched once. My wife held her up to me and we rubbed noses. I smelled of other men's cigars and she smelled of milk and soap.

Daughters are the antidote for sons. Sons are our own poor antidote for ourselves. My son Brighton causes and has caused in me every variant of concern, annoyance, irritation and disappointment that I, without him, would aim at myself. Good thing he knows it. A boy who rolls with the punches. He lets me know that he knows and we move ahead from there. But Helen since that night on the road has pulled and pushed me like a person drowning in the river. Sometimes I'm the one drowning and sometimes she is. Sometimes we both go down and for a moment, I don't know, but I think we reacquaint ourselves with the green light of life above us and kick towards that. I hope so. I have to put aside the part of Helen that's so much her mother it makes you forget. When I can do this I am worthy of my daughter, and may strive to be useful to her as I do with my son.

The night that changed our lives was not a star-spangled one. A miserly rain fell, and around midnight, when I left the party at Hal's and headed off to bed, some patchy ground fog hid my own driveway from me. I remember I had to back up and try again. This unsettled me more than it should have. I don't drink, hadn't been drinking, yet I was lost on my way home. I didn't like that.

I could not fall asleep for some time. I was bothered by one memory in particular which came back to me in such detail I almost didn't trust myself. When we were first married, my wife and I were invited to a party where we knew no one but our host's sister, and we did not know her well. She was an acquaintance of my wife's, not a friend. Why we accepted I don't remember. The party was not in full swing when we arrived that evening because it had been going on for days. Chairs were upturned and the floor was littered with food. Young men and their girls were asleep in corners, wrapped in each other, or leaning heavily against one another in the center of the room, apparently dancing. The room was large and bare and dark, lit by medieval torches spewing black smoke. A radio played faint and scratchy music. Our host came feebly to greet us, looking green and wearing his girl's pocketbook around his neck. She followed him like a kitten, mewing at him and batting at his shirttails with her high-heeled shoes which she wore on her hands. After they left I said to Tommie that I would like to take her home. She surprised me by saying that she wasn't ready to go home, we'd just arrived. She thought she would try and meet some people at this party, that's what parties were for. She got herself something to drink and I followed her around the room as she searched for alert bodies to engage with. There were none. But there was a whole crew outside, we could hear them hooting and jumping in the lake whose view the house commanded. We walked to the bottom of a steep lawn lit by spotlights and found another party going on at the dock. My wife's acquaintance was there holding court in the nude. She wore a party hat and I said happy birthday. She replied that it wasn't her birthday but somewhere in the world it was someone's. I again offered to take Tommie home, but she declined. There was an excitement in her I had never seen before. She looked around her quickly and sharply, like a dog in a chicken coop happy to have all the time in the world and no lack of choice. She wanted everyone to love her, that was my feeling, and she was certain they would and if they did not she could make them. I have never said this in my life and I will never say it again, but in that moment I became frightened of my wife to the point, almost, of hating her.

She would not go home and would not go home and finally, in exhaustion, I walked back to the car and lay down on the back seat with my legs out the door. My feelings for my wife had changed that night. I felt sorry for myself when in fact I might have felt sorry for her. I wanted to sleep — I need my sleep — and wake up somewhere other than this place of natural beauty and human chaos. But I only napped briefly, feeling too hot and cramped to sleep well, and too unsettled. I felt suddenly I had lost control of my life because I could not make my wife come home. It was a raw and ugly realization. It made me want to have nothing to do with her. In fact, it made me want to hurt her.

A girl drowned in the lake that evening. We didn't hear about it until much later. She was the wife of a fellow who wrapped himself in a corner with somebody else. That was the story. It was certainly possible. I think I know who the girl was. I had wandered away from the dock at one point and down the rocky shore a hundred yards or so, and I saw someone standing out in the water beyond the line of light from the house, out there at the beginning of the darkness, which felt like the beginning of safety. She, if it were she, stood to her waist in the lake, brushing the surface of it with her hands as if to clear a path for herself through it. And soon after, that's what she did. My reaction to the news of her drowning was disappointment that she had succumbed to the infidelity of her foolish husband and traded all her potential for death. I have been unfaithful to my wife on more than one occasion and am content that I am not worth drowning for. And this girl seemed to have an imagination. I saw it in her. I had wanted to walk out and stand there too.

When my wife might have died, when I sat as a passenger in my neighbor's car and approached the possibility of her death, I had only one thought in my head and that was for Helen. Or more accurately, it was for me. It was the fury of having given up another daughter. When I saw the wreck of the Volvo, its attendant police cars and ambulance, I thought, for this spectacular carelessness I have let my second one go. I wanted to tear the car apart with my own hands. I wanted to smash what was left of its glass and flatten it like a tin can and throw it behind me where I would not have to be reminded of my own violence nor its futility.

Brighton was home in bed, asleep in his underwear. I suddenly wanted him with me. We pulled him into our bed after Faith died — every night for a year after she died — his body finding the parts of us that were lost. I wanted to be found now. Helen's voice found me. I went to her and took hold of her and was aware and ashamed of never having hugged her before. Why do we wait? Why did I wait? She felt good and familiar, then quickly like someone frightened beyond what they can bear. She told me her mother had not died. I said, I know, I know, though I did not know. I found out later she didn't know either. It was only her prayer.

So we won that night. We did. For a while it looked like a terrible mess. Losing often looks neater and cleaner. But we won. We got everyone back. We lost parts of them afterwards, we lost whole bodies for a while, but their lives remained and remain an indisputable fact. The lungs heave, the heart pounds. My wife and two of my children exist. I don't express myself to them as I should. I am not brave enough to thank them. But I feel these things.

Hal

Tommie left us in one way, Helen in another. My heart, if it must be said, went to Helen. Tommie I knew. I knew the design of her earlobe, the warmth of her thigh, the whip of her tongue. I knew her desires, including those for death, for self-destruction. Helen I knew in form, a form like her mother's. And I knew the parts of her that were like parts of me. But what she wanted I did not know. At some point this amounts to who we are. Tommie and I were old love. Helen and I were courtship.

I wanted, during that terrible summer, to head her towards Frank. To lead her out of the wilderness of Tommie and into the valley of her father. But I didn't know how. Faint heart, Hal Chapin. I wanted to tell her the story of Tiny, but I thought she would mock my sense of connection to her. I was afraid of Helen. Her losses seemed to be mounting and she counted me among them. I didn't know exactly how I'd disappointed her, but I guessed that the man in my bed was part of it.

Sometimes in the early morning, five or six o'clock, if I was up getting a glass of water, I'd see her cross the field between us, swim goggles in hand. Behind me, Jody in the bed. Before me, Tommie's child. She swam every day of the summer before she went to work. A different kind of swimming than before, a rigorous workout with kickboard and a mile of laps. If I were feeling nostalgic I would groggily take myself into the guest bedroom overlooking the pool and sit on the bed and watch her. But it never did me any good. It was like watching Tommie drink. I can tell you how she was in the water, how she spun through it, weightlessly devouring it, slapping her legs down briskly at each end in perilous flipturns. But the point is there was no pleasure in it. An old hedonist like myself could see that. This long, wet exercise was a punishment for sins committed by the mother. Sins which were not sins.

She would have hated to know I watched her. She would have found somewhere else to swim. Eventually, when I woke at that hour I avoided the window. I put my feet on the floor, walked to get water and walked back again, not letting my mind wander to the mental turmoil in my pool. Once I imagined myself in a summer bathrobe, standing at the deep end, talking to her as she hurtled back and forth. I was the hand reaching to pet the animal, its wildness — not its wildness, its sorrow — caged. Helen, I said. I didn't say it, but saw myself saying it. I saw the words fly from my mouth and land like a ring on the blue water, an O of buoyancy through which she surfaced and was gone as the line connecting us played out.

After the divorce, when Dad still lived in Florida, Mom sent us down to stay with him one Christmas vacation. She put us on the train at Penn Station. My brother Thomas was in charge of suitcases and my sister Louise was in charge of me, though I was a great big eleven-year-old, as big as she was. My job was to lug around the basket of cold chicken, bread and butter sandwiches, a thermos of black bean soup and a thermos of cocoa. "You make sure they eat, Tiny." Tiny was my nickname at the time.

My mother was the last one off the train that day, the last well-wisher. She sat on the edge of the bed, the bottom berth in our compartment, smoking and staring out the window at the lightless station. "I think you and Louise should sleep here and Thomas up top," she said to me. "It's up to you." She continued to look out the window as a whistle blew frantically.

Thomas said, "You better go, Mom." He was fifteen and our spokesman.

"I will. I'll just wait here another minute." She looked a-round at the three of us. "I'll be sad without my babies."

"Mom, we're not babies," said Louise. She was fourteen.

"Tiny is," said Thomas.

Suddenly we all felt the first lurch of readiness, the train wheels unlocking, and I couldn't stand it any longer. "Mom, go," I pleaded, tugging on her arm. I was in tears and aware of Thomas and Louise and even my mother laughing.

"Tiny wants to get rid of me," she said.

"I don't!" But I had visions of her having to jump from the moving train, missing the platform, falling onto the tracks and under the wheels of our own car as we watched. How could I explain that I wanted her to go because I loved her and couldn't bear her death?

I remember almost every minute of that trip. The sight of the Capitol building all lit up in the night as we passed through Washington, D.C. The gentle rocking of the train that threw me and Louise against each other as we slept, or tried to. Thomas's snoring. Louise's very unboyish smell which I'd never noticed before. The morning rain obscuring the Carolinas. We ate breakfast in the dining car, thick slices of French toast with powdered sugar. I wandered from one end of the train to the other, making friends with the black porters who called themselves "colored." At one point in the long haul through Georgia I sat reading in our compartment. Louise was with me, also reading, and Thomas was off pursuing a girl he'd met at breakfast. I put my book down and said, "Why doesn't Dad live in Georgia?"

"Because he lives in Florida."

"I think this is the most beautiful state."

"You would."

"Don't you?"

"Do you mind, Tiny? I'm trying to read."

"Do you think he'll be governor someday?"

"No."

"I do. Do you even remember what he looks like?"

"Yes, now shut up."

"What if he looks different and we don't recognize him?"

"He knows what we look like. He's seen pictures."

"Why didn't we ever visit him before?"

"Because he lives in Florida and we live in New York."

"Maybe he didn't want to see us."

"Maybe."

"Do you like him, Louise? I don't think Thomas likes him."

"I said shut up, so shut up."

"I don't even remember him."

We arrived in Jacksonville that evening. Dad was not the dread stranger, but someone I almost knew. I was polite to him, the way I was to all my mother's friends. One of the first things I said was, "Thank you very much for all the money." He always sent us five dollars at Christmas. He burst out laughing, just he alone, and I realized it was the first time in my life in my family I didn't feel ganged up on by laughter.

He talked almost all the way to Tallahassee while the three of us took turns sleeping. I sat in the front seat and Thomas and Louise sat in the back. "How's your mother?" he asked me.

"Fine."

"How's that job of hers?"

"It's okay."

"You're in what grade now?"

"Sixth. Louise is in ninth and Thomas is in the fourth form. That's what they call tenth grade at the school he goes to."

"I know that," said my father. "You know how I know that?"

"How?"

"I went to that school myself."

"You did?"

"I went to a few different schools, but that's where I started out."

"Did you like it?"

"It was the happiest year of my life."

"Why didn't you stay, then?"

"I never stayed anywhere, especially if I was happy."

I rolled down the window to let a bee out. I hadn't seen a bee for months. "So maybe you were happy with us."

Dad started to say something but the rush of air woke Thomas who sat up and said, "Tiny, you pinhead, shut the stupid window." He fell back against the seat again and we were quiet, Dad and I. Now and then he'd point out an animal by the side of the road, mostly possums whose eyes went red in the headlights. If I couldn't see them as we passed, I said I could anyway. It was nothing. It was a dark shape against the dark underbrush that anyone could make up.

I liked Tallahassee. We stayed there for three days. It was warm, it was full of sweet-smelling bushes with blossoms the size of my two hands. The people there were slow and cordial, the women syrupy and coiffed. I'd never seen so many Negroes. They, like the porters on the train, called themselves colored and even nigger, and when they spoke among themselves they spoke in a code of quick high sounds like laughter, like a meltdown of my long, careful white northern speech. I couldn't understand a word of it. My father lived on a street of live oaks in a low brown house. The house next door had columns along the face of it and worn brick verandas, and in the morning an old Negro gardener raked the gravel driveway. I don't remember much about Dad's house. It was dark inside and he had a Victrola which we listened to all day long. He had a cook named Olympia, a tall, thin, light brown woman who came in in the morning and left at night. She was strict with all of us, even with Dad. She called him Mr. Tom. She called us Mr. Thomas, Miss Louise and Mr. Tiny. Dad didn't like the name Tiny and he called me Hal.

We went to Georgia to visit a friend of Dad's from New York, a man named Mr. Armstrong who owned a hunting plantation. That's where we spent most of that vacation, with the Armstrongs and their three daughters and another guest called Penelope Houghton who was there, I guess, for Dad to fall in love with. She was about ten or fifteen years younger than he was, a young woman in her twenties, and by my eleven-year-old reckoning, really more suited to me than Dad. Anne Armstrong, the daughter I was assigned to, was mature in a frightening way. She was aggressive, and I pretended to be bored by her, and pretty soon Thomas picked her up and I was free to court Penelope.

The plantation house was a three-story white brick mansion with high-ceilinged rooms and two large kitchens and an entire wing for servants. I'd never seen such a house. I was lost every time I set foot in it. My room was on a long hall of rooms on the second floor. Louise's room was next to mine and we shared a bathroom. The three Armstrong girls had rooms on that hall, and Thomas lived somewhere else, possibly on the third floor. He and I communicated almost not at all that week. It was a luxury for both of us.

At mealtimes we were waited on by black servants wearing black uniforms and white aprons, carrying platters of northern food. Roast beef, green beans, scalloped potatoes, soufflés. Or duck and quail, whatever we'd killed the day before, cooked in wine and blood. It took me several days to dare to go into the kitchen, but finally I did one afternoon and there was the staff, as Mrs. Armstrong called them, seated around a table piled high with the most delicious-smelling greasy meats and vegetables, everything cooked with pork fat and sugar and smothered with thick, floury gravy. I must have been drooling but I wasn't invited to sit down. I felt I'd seen something I shouldn't have. I was shy anyway around servants, especially blacks who were so much one way with each other and another way with white people. The only person I told about it was Penelope. I told her that night at dinner where I often sat next to her and even pulled her chair out for her if Dad didn't get there first. She made a face and said, "You mustn't pity them, Tiny. They're poor people. Their diet is poor. They can't help it. But all the money in the world couldn't change their ways. Negroes are proud. They're stubborn and proud and two-faced and they hate white people, there's not one who doesn't." She stabbed a bit of meat with her fork. "Isn't this a lovely chop?"

We went out shooting every day. I was given a 4.10 shotgun and allowed to shoot pine cones out of the tall slash pines around the house. When I could do that well enough I practiced on clay pigeons. The first living thing I shot was a mourning dove on Christmas day. I didn't care for guns. I didn't like the noise or the kick, though the 4.10 was a good size for me and when I learned to hold it properly it didn't kick at all. Penelope was an ace shot. Even Mr. Armstrong, who was a good shot himself, said so. His wife didn't shoot. If we were hunting quail, she brought her needlepoint and watched through binoculars from the mule-drawn wagon we rode in. Dad had a 12-gauge shotgun. It was a beautiful gun and I never heard him say a word against it, but he was a timid, erratic shot. Thomas would have nothing to do with weapons, and Louise shared a gun with the three Armstrong girls, but they weren't interested in whacking around in thick briars to kill small birds. They usually went riding and Thomas went with them.

When we went out on the wagon I sat up front with the driver, a man called Esau Jones. His skin was so black, in a certain light it looked blue. Dad and Penelope sat in the seat behind us, and Mr. and Mrs. Armstrong sat behind them. A second wagon carried the dogs, six or eight yelping pointers with bloody tongues. Esau's brother Edgar drove that wagon, and every now and then when the barking hit a certain pitch, he'd turn and lash the side of the cage with his mule whip.

For Christmas Dad gave me a tent and I pitched it under the slash pines. Thomas gave me his school tie and Louise gave me a fat book called *Gone with the Wind*. Penelope gave me and everyone else a box of peppermints. I gave her a box of pralines and some toilet water Louise helped me pick out. Dad, Thomas and Louise also got pralines, and the Armstrongs got nothing. At the last minute I thought of Olympia in Tallahassee, and with the money I had left I bought her a framed picture of a couple of swans on a lake with a castle in the background. At the top, written on a cloud, was the word *Inverness.*

I was a strange kid, a lonely kid. One hot afternoon when the scent was no good and the dogs just trailed behind the wagon begging water, and cowered and lay down when Edgar aimed his whip at them, Mr. Armstrong called an early end to the day and the adults came home and napped. Thomas, Louise and the Armstrong girls were out riding. I felt enervated but mentally restless. I lay in my tent and read *Gone with the Wind.* I was a fast reader and that book was disappearing too quickly. After a while I put it aside. I ate a peppermint, letting it slowly dissolve on my tongue, then I got up and went into the house and upstairs to my room, but on the threshold an unhappy noise stopped me. It was the sound of somebody crying and it came from a room at the end of the hall, Penelope's room. I was stealthy, and I walked towards the noise which was low and quiet and as if from deep in the throat. It frightened me to think of her alone in there with her sorrow. I had a feeling for her. I thought I was in love with her. That gave me the right to open her door and walk in and sit with her, give her comfort.

Her bed was a white, four-poster bed with a pink canopy, and she lay in it with my father, under my father, to be exact. I remember seeing his ass rise and fall and his white shirttail riding high up his back and her hands on his back. All I saw of her was her hands, then I closed the door.

In that hot weather we shot several rattlesnakes. We caught them asleep, sunning by their holes. They were diamondbacks, dark brown and mustard-colored, at least six feet long and thick as my calf. I'd never seen a live snake before and I thought they were beautiful. After Penelope shot the first one, Esau must have seen me crying. He gave me the reins and climbed down and cut off the rattles for me. He said dogs often died of snakebite, and he could remember a year when a mule did.

"How about a person?" I asked.

"No suh. Maybe a child but none that I know of."

"Do you have any children, Esau?"

"Yes suh. I have nine children, eight boys and a girl."

"What's your wife's name?"

He laughed for some reason. "Dosha Mae."

"Have you been married a long time?"

"Yes suh, a long time."

"If your wife died, would you marry somebody else?"

"Well now, suh, I'll have to think about that. I'll think about that and tell you tomorrow."

But we left the next day. Dad and Louise and I packed the car while Thomas kissed Anne Armstrong good-bye, off to one side but visible to all. It was a long, and as far as I could tell, smoldering kiss. Dad finally said, "Thomas."

We drove straight to Jacksonville. Again I was in the front seat and Thomas and Louise were in the back. It was a cool day, gray and foggy in little patches where the road ran close to a swamp. We passed pecan groves and bright green fields of what Dad said was winter rye. I asked him if he liked the South.

"You mean living here? I like living here."

"Would you ever move up north again?"

"I don't know. Maybe." We were just outside of Jacksonville. I think he knew I was trying to find a way of saying good-bye to him. The other two were sleeping, Louise with her mouth open and Thomas with his head on his own shoulder. "Look, Hal. I'll tell you something. It's got nothing to do with anything but it's something at least." He laughed. "How's that for a political speech?"

"I'd vote for you."

"You're a lot like me. You want people to like you. I think we like each other but it doesn't matter, okay? I'm going to lean on you, no matter what. That's what I'm trying to tell you. And you lean on me, go ahead, I want you to. That make sense?"

I nodded.

"You sure?"

"Yes."

"See this?" We were paralleling the river, passing a navy yard. "We're going to war, did you know that?"

"No."

"Yup, that's what all this is about. We're getting ready. You ever hear of Hitler?"

"Sure. I know him."

"Well, sooner or later we're going to jump right into Hitler's war. We can't stay out of it much longer. I think it'll be sooner. I hope so, you know why? Then you won't have to be in it."

I looked out the window at the gray ships. They were lined up like shoes in a closet. There wasn't a person in sight anywhere. "But Thomas will have to be in it," I said.

"Thomas won't do anything he doesn't want to do."

"I won't either."

But I knew he was right. I'd do anything, I'd go to war if it meant I'd be liked. I was a boy of yeses.

He put us on the train and I spent most of the trip pretending to read but really just thinking. About my father. About Thomas. About war. About Esau Jones. About the diamondback writhing by its hole, headless and tailless, more alive dead than most living things. About love. About Olympia. About Penelope Houghton. About her pink canopy bed and my father's white ass. Mom met us at the station and in a private moment away from Thomas and Louise I told her I didn't want to be called Tiny anymore.

"Oh, Tiny," she laughed, "don't be silly. You'll always be my Tiny."

"Dad called me Hal." Her face fell and I said quickly, "It's okay, Mom. You don't have to." I couldn't bear her disappointment any more than I could her death.

PART THREE

Helen

Brighton's plane was early, which I hadn't counted on. He was leaning against the wall by the gate, one foot up on the wall, waiting for me. He was in blue jeans and a white button-down shirt with a pale pink tie I'd given him for high school graduation. A pair of tortoise-shell glasses gave him an Atticus Finch look. He spotted me and came towards me, hands out, almost apologetic. "You're not late," he said, seeing the disappointment on my face. I feel like I've failed if I keep someone waiting. "You're right on time. We were early."

"How could you be early?"

"I don't know. I guess we just flew fast."

"Is that all you have, that bag?"

"This is it. And my jacket."

"That's the tie I gave you."

"This one? Yeah, it is. How are you?" He put his arm around me, a sideways hug.

He picked up his bag and we started walking through the terminal. "How is it back home?" I asked. "How's Dad?"

"Dad's good."

"Does he know you're out here?"

"You mean did I tell him?"

"Who else would tell him?"

"I don't know. No, I didn't tell him. It's just a few days. I think you ought to talk to him, Helen. I don't necessarily mean right away, but soon. He asks about you, and I don't always know what to say."

"If he wants to know about my life, he can ask me. He knows where I live. He knows where San Francisco is. He can call me."

"He wouldn't do that."

"He can write me a letter then."

"He's not good at that, Helen. He doesn't know how to talk to people."

"Yes, he does. He talks to you, and he used to talk to me."

"I know he'd like to see you is all. He worries about you. That's the last thing I'll say."

I stopped and turned to him. "Why does he send *you* to say it?"

"He didn't send me to say it. It's my own opinion." We started walking again. "He's scared of you, Helen. You remind him of Mom."

"Then he never knew her either."

We didn't talk much on our way into the city. "Are you tired? You must be wiped out," I said.

"I am, yeah. I think I'll just take a little nap. What time is it?"

"Eight. Eleven o'clock your time. Did you go to work today?"

"Yeah. Hal picked me up at work and took me to the airport. He goes to Connecticut every weekend. His mother's there."

"I know."

"He takes care of her. You okay driving? You need someone to keep you awake?"

I laughed. "Who would that be? Go ahead and drop off, this is your chance. I'm taking us out to eat, okay? Thai food?"

"Sure. Make it pink tie." He looked over at me. "Even half asleep I'm funny."

He propped up his bag like a big pillow. He took off his glasses and dropped his head forward and closed his eyes. He moved his hand over and rested it on my seat, next to my leg, giving me the choice. I took it and held onto it. I brought it into my lap and he gave me a squeeze before he went to sleep. I missed this. Most of the time I kept myself so sealed off from affection I had no chance to miss it. Brighton's visits always caused me this pleasure and this pain. It was new to both of us. Not new, but learned; nothing we'd grown up with. Growing up, I'd sooner shake hands with Tommie than hug her. She put out a vibration that stopped me about a foot from her skin. And Dad was impossible. Hal taught me affection. That was one of the things I resented him for when we became estranged, teaching me something I had no other place for. I still haven't found a home for it except with Brighton, and I only see him two or three times a year. It was the reason I was an athlete. It was why I did karate. To be physical with someone, with people, in a system defined by rules. I've always needed the rules. Brighton does better without them. He's Tommie in that way and I'm Dad.

In college I stopped being an athlete and became a nerd. There wasn't money for me in athletics, it was as simple as that. I also started sleeping with people. I was attracted to women, to their bodies. I'd spent so much time in locker rooms looking at bodies, it was my natural aesthetic. But for a lot of reasons I didn't want to go to bed with them. I didn't think I was gay. I didn't feel gay. Of course there was Tommie and that was complicated. I really wasn't free to sleep with women. Then one day I realized I'd never seen a man's body, not a naked man, so how was I to be attracted? It was faulty logic, but I lived in my head at the time.

I talked to a friend of mine, Jill, my best friend. She said she liked sleeping with men but their bodies were a little scary looking. "You have to like the equipment, you have to like what they can do." She suggested I find someone my size, preferably older, and not in any of my classes, and go off and do it. "Just do it. Don't expect miracles. It'll hurt. I'd do it in the dark if I were you. Men are different. Their bodies are hairy, you have to get used to them."

"They're hairy in the dark too, aren't they?"

"It's your life. Why add to the stress of the first time, that's all I'm saying. You've really never seen a man before? Where have you been? Don't you have a brother?"

I told her in my family we didn't even brush our teeth in front of each other. She said, "And when you peed you turned on the water to hide the noise, right? It's bad, Helen, but it's not hopeless. I've got someone in mind. Give me a day or two. Trust me. Do you trust me?"

I said I did.

Alan Wang was Jill's Comp. Lit. professor, and his wife, Sheila Harness, taught me anthropology my first semester at Santa Cruz. Sheila was a huge woman, big-boned, with a deep, emphatic voice. The human condition was a source of constant amusement to her, a perspective I badly needed at the time. I did well in her class. It was a small class, and she kept her distance from her students until they were no longer her students. When it was over, she and I began to cultivate a friendship.

At first it was all about anthropology, which I'd decided to major in. We met here and there, in her office or over coffee at the Whole Earth Restaurant on campus. She talked and I listened. We knew very little that was personal about each other. I knew she liked me and I was happy to be liked. I was a good student. I hadn't always been, and that in itself was a thrill.

One day on a whim I tracked her down for lunch. I stopped by her office. She was in conference with a student. "Oh, Helen," she said. "Did we have an appointment today?" She turned to the student. "Excuse me, Mark."

"No," I shrugged. "It's nothing. I just thought you might want to have lunch. You're busy. It's okay. We'll be in touch."

I started to leave and she said, "Lunch would be fine, Helen. I haven't eaten yet and I'm famished. Mark and I have another five or ten minutes."

Mark looked surprised. "But I'm scheduled until one-thirty."

She ignored this. "Come back at one, can you?"

I said that would be fine.

She drove me to a fish-and-chips place called The Wiggly Eel. It was a long, crowded room with dark walls and two ineffective ceiling fans. The only light came from the front window, and those of us at the back could barely read a menu. People sat in couples, predominantly male professors and female students, at round tables designed for two. I nodded at a few of the students before I realized that was the last thing they wanted — to be recognized.

We sat down and she said, "You don't drink in the afternoon, do you?"

"Not really. I don't really drink."

"Not even wine? I was going to suggest a glass of bad white wine with your lunch."

"What are you having?"

"Some bad red wine."

"I'll have that."

"With fish it will have to be white."

We ordered. She asked me where I was from. She asked about my family. She was digging, doing her research. It was different than any other conversation we'd had. I said my father lived in New Jersey, my brother was at NYU. "You have a mother, don't you?" she said. "Have or had?"

"Had," I nodded.

"When did she die?"

"She didn't die. She went away."

"Went away? Where is she?"

"We don't hear from her. She left when I finished high school."

"This past year?"

"Yes, the day after I finished."

Dr. Harness leaned away from the table and lit a cigarette. Our meal came and she ate quickly, ravenously, her cigarette burning in the ashtray. She ordered another glass of wine for both of us, though I hadn't touched mine. "How's your food?" she asked. I said it was good and she said, "No one comes here for the food." She looked around distractedly.

I asked her if she was married.

"Yes. Does that surprise you?"

"Why would it?"

"Some people are against marriage. I am. So is my husband." I nodded as if that made sense to me. "We've had to reinvent the wheel in our marriage. We have an open relationship. We don't own each other, but we keep no secrets from each other either."

"Oh," I said. I watched her blow a coil of smoke up to the ceiling. "Do you have any children?"

"He's sterile." She stubbed out her cigarette. "Isn't that ridiculous? He's ten years younger than I am. You'd think the youthful little sperm could keep up with an old egg like mine, but apparently they don't swim fast enough. Weak tails, I don't know. I'm not crazy about children anyway. The disappointment is his. I've had my chances. It isn't my first marriage. That's what you did in my day, Helen. You married."

Suddenly she raised her glass. "To your mother, wherever she may be. What's her name?"

"Tommie."

"To Tommie."

I couldn't drink a toast to Tommie and I said so.

"Why?" asked Dr. Harness. "What has she ever done to you? You graduated, she graduated. Your life is yours and hers is hers. How old is she?"

"When I was fourteen, she was forty, so now she's forty-four."

"My age," she nodded. "You're looking at forty-four. Not quite the old hag, not yet, Helen." She laughed bitterly. "There are things I understand about your mother. She ran off with a lover, didn't she?" I looked at her blankly. "She did, didn't she? If you haven't heard from her she's with her lover. Why does that shock you? Women need a sexual life. We need a dance to do on our own grave. Listen to me, Old Mother Harness. I'll tell you something." She lowered her voice. "I'm more easily aroused now than I ever was in my teens or twenties or thirties. It's wonderful. Does that embarrass you? Look at me. Why should that embarrass you?"

I brought my head up. "I'm not embarrassed," I said.

"Then look at me. Are you jealous?"

"No. I mean, of what?"

"Envious?"

"Dr. Harness, I — "

"Sheila, Helen. Please." Suddenly she seemed genuinely hurt. Her body relaxed. She slumped back in her chair. "We haven't understood each other, have we? I thought we were," she searched for a word, "together somehow. Tied. Seeing things the same way. We're not, are we? Maybe you've had enough. Maybe that's enough for one day."

I said I thought it was.

Neither of us spoke for a minute or two. I was suddenly aware of the heat and noise of the restaurant, currents of conversation overlaid with the smell of fried fish and mustard and vinegar. Finally she said, "You'll come out again, won't you, Helen? Have I disturbed you? I haven't pried, have I?"

"No."

"Good. Very few people are willing to be honest. I hope you'll always be honest with me."

"I'll try," I said.

"Don't try. Try is a weak word."

We drove back up the hill to the campus. At the parking lot she asked, "You don't have a car, do you?"

I said I did, why?

"It might be nice to drive somewhere next time. You could meet me at my house. We could go somewhere away from people. Up to the hills. Or who knows? We might want to stay home and sit on my comfortable sofa. How does that sound?"

I said it sounded good, it sounded fine. I was pretty busy.

"We're all busy, Helen. I know how busy you are." She took

my hand. "You're not frightened, are you? You're not frightened of me?"

I said I wasn't.

"Good. My husband has his own life, by the way. We don't bother each other."

I said I'd be happy to meet him.

"You wouldn't need to meet him," she said. "Do you like men, Helen?"

"Yes. I mean, I guess. Sure I like them."

"No one in particular?"

"No."

"But you've slept with men?"

"Not exactly, no."

"I see. But you'd like to?"

"I haven't thought about it very much. I just know I'm going to."

"Quite the fatalist, my dear. You sound like I did when I was your age, but that was a different era. It surprises me. You come from such a civilized generation, such a sexually free one."

"I guess."

"You guess. Life is a great experiment. Your crowd understands this."

"I think you appreciate it more than I do, to tell you the truth."

"You'll appreciate it." She opened her door and got out, and I did too. "Your life hasn't begun yet."

After that afternoon I put a red circle around Sheila Harness, a mental warning. I didn't search her out. I rarely saw her. I missed her intelligence, but not her aggression. I was surprised she didn't get in touch with me. I was relieved, but also somewhat disappointed. That spring was a lonely one for me. The human condition was anything but amusing. That's when I talked to my friend Jill whose counsel was Just do it, Helen. She did, as promised, come up with someone to do it with. That someone, by extraordinary coincidence, was Alan Wang.

"It's impossible," I told her. "I can't, Jill. I know his wife."

"Everyone knows his wife, that's the point."

"Well, she's a good teacher. She's popular."

"In the biblical sense, stupid. They do a lot of fucking, both of them. She goes both ways, but he's fairly tame. He's an older man, I mean older than you. He's attractive, not too tall, not too big, not too hairy. Wang. You know, he's Chinese."

"I don't like it."

"You don't have to like it. You have to get it over with. Alan would be a good one for that. She doesn't have to know, Helen. I'm sure they don't discuss their lovers."

I was sure they did. In the end I know that's why I said yes to it. I'm not proud of that moment in my life, but she was Tommie and I wanted to twist the knife.

We met, Alan and I, at a Comfort Inn. Neither of us noted the irony, at least not aloud. I was too nervous to be funny, and he wasn't nervous enough. I never got to know him well, but he seemed like the kind of man who never lost his reserve, never made a joke, never really let go. It would be dishonorable. Fucking his wife's ex-student was not dishonorable. I don't know what it was for him.

We took our clothes off. He looked at his watch. We lay down next to each other on one of the queen-size beds. He stiffened, not just his penis, his whole body. He stroked my sides. He reached down and rubbed me and asked if that felt good. I said yes, even though it was too much, it hurt. Finally he got on top of me and pushed his penis inside me. To him I must have felt like a piece of wood, trying to be still, trying to

[172]

go unnoticed, trying to feel if there was anything I liked about any of this. He rolled back and forth so our hips clacked together like stones. He burrowed into me and when I thought of him that way, like a little animal burrowing, I could feel some pleasure, like the pleasure of stroking a cat. He rocked for a while, then at some mysterious point reared up on his arms with his head back and laughed. He collapsed on top of me and I thought I'd killed him.

Finally he moved. He asked if I was finished and I said yes. He reached down and rubbed me anyway, and I thought, this is better. This is nice. This is a lot better. It was a strange orgasm, the first I'd ever had with another person watching. We dressed and walked outside together and said good-bye.

Driving back to school I thought only of practical things. An exam coming up. A paper due. A long overdue letter to Brighton. I knew the letter wouldn't include the afternoon's activity. Not yet. Maybe not ever. I knew the next man I slept with would be someone easy, someone unmarried, someone my age. It wouldn't take place in a motel. It would be in the light, in the morning, in a bed slept in by us. I didn't need to love him, but I wanted to like him. I'd have to organize some birth control.

I live on Washington Street, east of Van Ness. My apartment is small and dark, in the back on the second floor. Not everyone in San Francisco lives at the top of a hill in a high-ceilinged, sunlit room with a view of the bay. There's a down side to paradise.

We got in late Friday night after the Thai dinner and woke up Saturday morning with no food in the house. Nothing. A jar of instant coffee and some Coffeemate. Brighton got dressed to go to the store. It was a beautiful spring day and I said, "Let's walk around the city a little today."

"Yeah, I'd like to. I should get some stuff for sandwiches. I'll make tuna fish sandwiches. We can take them with us."

"That's dumb," I said. "If you want a sandwich we'll get a sandwich somewhere. The city has sandwiches."

"It's easy to make them."

"Then we have to carry them."

"I'll carry them."

"Let's just eat out."

"Okay," he said. He was standing at the door, about to go shopping. "We'll eat out." He looked at the floor. "We're always eating out, Helen. We ate out last night. You said tonight we're going to some Japanese place. I just . . . " He shrugged. "Never mind."

"You just what?"

"It's expensive. I don't want you paying for me all the time."

"Paying for you is easy. I like paying for you. You're a cheap date." I laughed.

"I'm everybody's cheap date."

"I was kidding."

"No, I am. Really. I'm like a wife or something. I mean it's not bad to be a wife, I'm not saying that. If you want to be a wife, be a wife. But I don't want to be." He knew what I was thinking. "Not just Hal. He pays for food and stuff, but I do more than half the cooking. That's fair. I don't mind cooking. And I pay him a little rent for my room, which he could use. It's a big apartment. But Dad. Dad calls up and wants to take me to the Channel 13 barbecue. He calls up a month in advance. It'll be all his cronies and their wives and me. What can I say? I can't say no." He shook his head. "I feel like this is somebody else's life and I don't know how I got here. Sometimes at work I think, what am I doing proofreading this stuff? I should've written it. I'm almost twenty-eight years old. I was this kid full of promise, I was smart. Even my shrink said I was smart. I was smarter than him sometimes. I had some pretty all right friends, like Maria. She and her friends were these interesting, smart people. We thought about the world a lot. We were hopeful and philosophical and, I don't know, just hopeful." He looked around the room, my tiny, grubby, dark living room off a dark, grubby street in San Francisco. "We had something," he said. "I think you have it, but I lost it. I'm glad you have it, Helen, I really am. I just wish I had it too. I don't know if I ever will again. It's sad."

"What's sad is that you think that way, that's what's sad."

"What do you mean?"

"Look at this pit. Take a good look at this motel room. This is where I live." I picked up one of the lamps that came with the place. Cheap lamps, a couple of end tables, an armchair from the New Jersey house and one twin bed in the bedroom — that was the meaning of "furnished." "The only thing you've lost is your powers of discernment. What do I have that you don't have? I have a job because I need something to keep me busy so I won't have time to think about my life, my life that has no one in it; I mean no one, Brighton. No one close to me except the people I work with, and we're close the way a dog team is close. I come home after work and you know what I do? I go to bed. I wake up in the morning and you know what I do? I go to work."

"You need a boyfriend."

"Sure I need a boyfriend. Can I buy a boyfriend? You're telling me you think I have it. If you mean money, sure, I've got money. I don't spend it. I spend a little on clothes. What else am I going to spend it on? Go to the movies alone? It gets old."

"You could get some furniture."

"Thanks."

"You need some furniture."

"Brighton, I'm lonely!"

I threw the lamp at him. It was a white, studded glass lamp. I didn't think or aim, I just lashed out. It hit him in the shin and bounced to the floor without breaking. He leaned down and touched his leg, feeling the edges of the bruise, wincing. He set the lamp upright and backed away from me, looking at the floor, favoring his good leg. He let himself out the door and I didn't see him again until late afternoon when he came home with the makings of dinner. He made lamb chops he must have paid his life for, and boiled potatoes with parsley, and fresh green beans. After we ate, I said I was going in to work, and he said fine. I came home around midnight. He was asleep on his makeshift bed on the living room floor, his book on his chest.

I was up the next morning before he was. I ate the leftover green beans and was making myself a cup of instant coffee when he wandered into the kitchen, wearing pajama bottoms and a T-shirt. He was scratching his neck, digging at it, raising welts. It was an old morning habit of his.

"I can't watch you do that," I said.

He looked sleepy and disoriented. "Do what?"

"Scratch your neck."

"Oh. Sorry. I don't even know when I'm doing it." He looked at my cup and said, "I bought some real coffee. I'll make you some real coffee. Don't drink that stuff, it's garbage."

"I like it."

He shrugged. "Okay. You want breakfast? I got some muffins. And bacon. I can make up some bacon."

"I had the green beans."

I watched him make his breakfast. In that miserable kitchen he moved like an athlete in chains. It took him only a moment to catch his stride, to find his grace. Coffee water boiling, muffin heating in the oven. A plate of sliced apples and cheese appeared out of nowhere. It was all ready at the same time. He carried it out to his bed on the floor and sat down cross-legged. "What are we doing today?" he asked. "What's the plan?"

"I'm going in to work."

He looked at me. Without his glasses on, his face had a startled look. "It's Sunday," he said softly. "Lay off, Helen. Don't be an asshole."

"The world doesn't stop because it's Sunday."

"It stops for you every time you go to work."

"That's deep."

"Look," he said. "I'm leaving on Tuesday. Tomorrow's Monday. This is it. This is the only day. Tomorrow you go to work and I go see Roger." Roger was a college friend of his. Brighton always called him when he came to the city and they got together for an evening or a cup of coffee or a walk.

"I thought he was married," I said. "Didn't he just get married?"

"A couple of months ago."

"You're still going to see him?"

"Well, yeah."

"Does his wife know?"

He looked at me strangely. "Know?"

"About Roger. She's married to a gay man. Don't you think that's something people need to know? I'd want to know it."

"Why? What difference does it make? Everybody has a history."

"Not every man has a history of male lovers."

"Most men do."

"Then you're all gay."

He didn't say anything. He took his plate to the kitchen. He came back into the living room and I was standing by the window, looking into the alley which for some reason that morning was littered with vegetables, maybe a spill from the back of a produce truck. "I'm going to get dressed now," he said. When I didn't move, he went over and got some clothes out of his bag: clean underwear, socks, a clean T-shirt. He pulled out some more T-shirts and refolded them and put them back in his bag. He made his bed, piling the blankets in a corner out of the way. I wondered how long it would take him to tell me to get out and give him some privacy while he dressed. I realized it would take longer than I wanted to wait.

"You're not going to take a shower?" I asked.

"I had a bath last night. Why?"

"I was just wondering. You always take a shower in the morning."

"Well, I'm going to skip it."

"You're the cleanest person I know." I didn't turn from the window. "You just have to ignore me. When I say stuff like that, ignore it, okay? The stuff about Roger. It doesn't mean anything. It means I'm sick of myself."

"I know."

"I spend a lot of time being sick of myself. I don't know how to change it. I don't have anybody to talk to except when you come. I'd like to see Tommie. I'm ashamed to say that. Do you ever want to see her?"

"Sometimes."

"What do you do?"

"I go see her."

"You see her?" I turned around.

"Yeah."

"Where is she?"

"She's in Vermont. For a while she lived in Oregon, but now it's Vermont."

"And you didn't tell me?"

He shook his head. "I was pretty sure you didn't want to know."

"I'm glad you didn't tell me. It's strange. I used to know everything about her. Now I can't feel her at all."

"That's good, Helen. That's better."

"What's she like?"

"She's got these pretty bad seizures. She's had them since the accident, but she didn't tell anyone. You probably knew."

I nodded. "Is she with someone?"

"You mean, like a girlfriend?" He laughed. "It's the wrong word. Mom with a girlfriend."

It was the first time I hoped she was with someone. "A lover," I said. "Call it that."

"She's in this sort of community. It's all women there. They grow stuff and live there and, you know, I guess they go to bed with each other. It's corny. The whole place is pretty corny. When I go see her we have to meet in the town because there's no men on the land. The women have beards and shit. Mom's funny about them. She says she won't be there forever, she just needs a place to be for now. With the seizures she has to be around people."

"Does Dad know where she is?"

"Yeah. He was the one who told me. They keep in touch. They're not against each other or anything." He looked at me and read my mind. "She's not against you, Helen."

We talked all morning. Starting with Tommie — she'd vanished for seven years; she was worth an hour of our time — and moving on to everything you can think of. Brighton's love life — on hold — his friendship with Hal, his boredom with Dad and his dread of hearing Tommie's voice on the phone, drunk and disoriented, apologetic or cynical. He was the one she called when remorse got the best of her. If Hal answered, she hung up.

"Has Dad seen her?" I asked. I was stretched out on the living room floor in my pajamas. Brighton was in his pajamas, sitting in the chair.

"Not yet. They talk on the phone."

"He hates the phone."

"She calls him, usually. There's one phone for the whole community. You never get her, it rings in someone else's cabin or teepee or whatever, and they have to go get her. Dad can't deal with that. He can't really deal with anything. I think it would be very strange being married to him. He's scared of everything."

"I'm waiting for him to find a girlfriend."

"He won't. It won't help."

"They really have teepees?"

"I don't know."

"Mom in a teepee." I shook my head and laughed.

"She looks good," said Brighton. "Well, she's thin."

"She's always been thin."

"Thinner. She looks older but happier. Not really happier, but not so pissed off."

"She's still drinking," I said.

"Well, yeah."

"I think she'll come back. Do you?"

"Come back?"

"To live."

"With Dad, you mean?"

I nodded.

"I don't think so."

"I do," I said. "I think so." But it didn't have the strength of a premonition for me, it was just a thought.

In the afternoon we got dressed and went out and walked around Golden Gate Park. People were out in shorts and T-shirts, throwing frisbees. We came home and took naps. Brighton made sandwiches and we drove to the beach to watch the sun go down.

"It does this every day," I said.

"Yeah. Back east too. Every day."

We watched it hit the rim and flatten, like someone spreading marmalade on toast.

"I don't think you'll live there much longer," I said.

"I don't know. I don't know about the city. When Hal's mother dies he'll move to Connecticut. I don't know where I'll go. We'll see."

"I think you'll go back to school."

"You do?"

"You're brainy. You're much brainier than I am."

"No, I'm not. I was just a lonely kid so I got along well with books. I love books. I don't read them anymore but I still love them."

"You read them all day long, it's your job."

"That's different."

"I used to be a jock, same thing. I don't do a damn thing now except sit at my desk and eat lunch."

"You have a good body, Helen. You're lucky."

"I'm flabby."

"No, you're not. You're very muscular."

I pinched my arm. "This. This is flab."

"Flex. See, it's muscle tone."

I laughed.

We drove back to my apartment. I wasn't used to napping in the afternoon and now I felt restless. I asked Brighton if he wanted to go to a movie. He said no, he thought he'd go out for a while.

"I'll go with you," I said. He gave me a pained look. "Okay, I won't." I took off my coat and sat down in the armchair and watched him get ready. He went into the bathroom and closed the door. I heard him brushing his teeth and peeing.

He came out and put on a clean shirt and asked, "Where's your iron?"

"I don't trust it, it's got a funny smell."

"Does this look really bad, this shirt?"

"It looks like you slept in it."

He went and stood in front of the long mirror on the bedroom door. "It's not that bad."

"The other one was better."

"Screw it, I'm not going to change it. I can't wear a dirty shirt."

He ran his fingers through his hair. He raised his chin and moved his head back and forth, eyeing the mirror, looking for flaws. It wasn't the first time I'd watched him get ready for a night prowl; he often went out by himself at night. But this vanity was new. I didn't know if I liked it. It used to be he just looked the way he looked, now he cared about how he looked and it made him less attractive. It made him less fresh, less appealing. I could see where one day it would take him away from me and put him in the hands of I wasn't sure what. His own tribe, I suppose, but it felt like death and decay.

He wasn't even thirty. He was a young man, he still looked like a young man, but living in San Francisco I'd seen enough of who my brother might become. The gay men. They weren't like Hal. They were more like Hell's Angels. Some of them were like Hal. Prissy, soft, stuffed into their clothes. They touched their heads a lot, worried about every lost hair. You'd see them in restaurants, in couples, whispering to each other, backbiting, rolling their eyes, folding their hands, acting. I felt very unattractive around them, very used by them. I don't need men to flirt with me in order to feel good about myself, but I like people to see who I am before they dismiss me.

"Tomorrow I'm getting you an iron," said Brighton. He put on his pink tie. "What do you think you'll do tonight?"

"I don't know. Read or something."

"That sounds good."

"No, it doesn't. What are you going to do?"

"Probably just walk around. I don't really feel like I'm here yet. I'll probably just walk around and try and kind of land."

"Does that mean go have sex with people?"

He glanced at me in the mirror. "Not necessarily."

"When you go out is that what you usually do?"

"Sometimes. There's places to go just for sex. I don't go there. I mostly go where I can dance. If I like someone, we'll have sex."

"Does it feel good?"

"Sure." He left the mirror and came and stood in the middle of the room. "You mean sex?"

"With someone you don't know."

"Yeah. It feels fine."

After he left I got into bed with a junky novel and thought about him. He was simpler than I was. So was every man I'd ever met, certainly every man I'd ever slept with, starting with Alan Wang. Dad was simpler than Tommie. It must have driven her crazy. She was complicated and screwed up and she wanted everything; she was very devouring. He wanted a quiet, normal life. She must have driven him crazy too. I could imagine them living together again as friends. Tommie could be a friend to men. What had happened between her and Hal had happened because she'd laid herself bare to him all her life, as if he were a

[183]

woman. She was much harder on women. And she was jealous. He'd taken her son.

I saw my brother as doomed. It was not a happy sight. I saw him walking the city to find sex, which was freedom to him. He was tired of being a wife. He was restless. This was good. At home he was living Tommie's life for her, as Hal's confidant and Dad's companion. He was the family ambassador, the boy who never grew up, who never left home. When he did, as he did on nights like this, he did it with the knowledge of the knife held close to his heart. Or so I imagined.

Brighton

I worry about Helen. She looks like hell these days, skinny and stringy like an outdoor cat, a sad outdoor cat. When I see her I have this feeling I'm the door of the house she wants to come into. She comes up to it and slides along it and starts to trust it, and then because the weekend's over I go away again and she does too.

A person needs to know they're wanted. Helen doesn't. Dad's worried about her. Mom's afraid of her. Hal has a conscience about her. He thinks he damaged her. You and everyone else, I say. They were close and then they weren't. Whose fault is that? No one's.

No, he says, it's someone's.

Then it's hers. She outgrew you.

She was jealous, Brighton, of you. Of my attention to you.

You think she didn't wake up one day and say, gee, what am I doing hanging out with this old guy and his boyfriend, I've got other fish to fry?

I don't think she did, says Hal.

Then think what you think.

I live with Hal. I have more or less since college. He moved into the city at that time and I was going to be a freshman at NYU. Dad laid this trip on me about money. He said I should think about living at home and commuting. Dad, I said, I'm nineteen years old. I'm not living at home and commuting. The best way to handle Dad, I discovered, was to be firm with him. He was scared of being home alone with Mom and Helen, that's what it was.

We were quite a family then. It had been a year of people holding their breath, ever since Mom came back from her summer on the road. She was different. I didn't know anything about the seizures then, I just knew she wasn't with us anymore, she was somewhere else. I was the only one who talked to her about her life. Everyone else, even Hal, who she'd been tight with for so long, treated her like she'd break if they said the word "why?" to her.

Once she talked about Jeanne Ann Love. She went and stayed with Jeanne Ann for some of that summer. Mom was experimenting with her lifestyle. She had these feelings and she took them right to Jeanne Ann and I guess she found out that feelings weren't enough to make the ship fly. She had us to consider. I said, think about how that makes me feel, to be the chain around your neck, me and Dad and Helen. She said, wait till you're my age, forty going on sixteen.

What does that mean?

It means I'm tired, Bright. It means a chain looks good to an old woman.

Oh, Mom. Come on.

Oh, Mom, come on, yourself. I don't know who I am, I don't know how to be in this family. I don't know what to do with myself. I'm lost, you can see that. Hold on to me. Do that for me, will you? Keep me here. I promise you, when it's time to do the wrong thing for the right reason, I'll do it. You'll know it, Brighton. I'll fly out of here. Maybe you won't hate me.

I couldn't stand it when she talked like that.

She said, of course, maybe you will.

It's hard to let a confused person just be confused, especially if it's your mother. I began to like Mom at this time. I began to like her courage. I could see she was walking along the edge of a great risk, and I more or less intentionally set out to follow her.

Hal's boyfriend Jody left him that fall and went to live with someone else. That was okay with me, he didn't like me. I don't think he liked anyone he couldn't borrow money from. But Hal was lonely. I hung out with him. It's funny, as I began to like Mom, I began not to like Hal. They were opposites at that time in their lives. She was coming from a feeling of constant emergency, like something in her was emerging. He was pulling this thick blanket over his loneliness and telling everybody, hey, I'm fine, I'm fine. She was full of choices, he was flat against the wall. I took a good look at that and said, who do I want to be here? It was the same question I was asking myself around Maria DiAngelo's bunch.

They were an amazing bunch. Maria was their centering force, she and her karate. I was their little experiment. I don't mean they did weird stuff to me. They didn't mess with my head. If anything, they cleaned up the mess in my head. What they were after was not about themselves — they wanted to shape a feminist man. It was strange, it was radical, but it was innocent. It was actually very intelligent on their part. They showed me how to touch women, for one thing. This was something I was scared of and not really very good at.

I did make love to one of Maria's friends once. Her name was Kit and she was in the group, but she was older, in her twenties. We did it privately, at her house. She did most of the work because even though I was mechanically all there, I was nervous and sort of dead inside. It wasn't steamy. I liked Kit. I thought I was attracted to her, so it was weird to get in her bed and not feel that pull, like you're being pulled along by your guts. In the beginning especially, sex is too strange if it's not steamy. Something else has to take over and with Kit nothing did. Then I did the worst thing, which was to apologize. I forget how she handled it. She was good, she was a nice woman. I was smart to pick an older woman. She wasn't insecure at all. Eventually she was the first person to put in my head the idea that I might be gay.

The next spring I graduated. Nine days later I started my summer job. I worked as an editorial assistant at a small publishing house called Cosmos Books. That was its last summer. The person I spent most of my time with was a guy named Peter. He was married and he had a new baby, a little girl. He and his wife Marcia and their baby lived over on York Avenue, up in the Eighties, in a one-bedroom apartment that had a real cockroach problem. At work Peter talked a lot about the cockroaches, and how you couldn't exterminate if you had a new baby, and how the new baby kept him up all night, and how many diapers she went through, and what was in the diapers. Eventually everything came around to the baby. You could start with the Ku Klux Klan and you'd get to the baby. Baseball, football, basketball, you'd end up with the baby. Woodstock happened that summer. It was all about the baby. It made a lot of people in the office crazy, but I liked it. I like babies. I at least like the idea of them.

One day I said, Peter, my man, when do I get to see this baby of yours? He couldn't believe it. Someone wanted to see his baby. We picked a time, a Friday, the next Friday afternoon after work. We took the subway uptown together and got off at Eighty-sixth and Lexington and walked over to York Avenue. His apartment building was new. It was white brick. It looked cheaply built to me but I'm no architect. Also, you don't tell the father of a new baby that his building looks like it's about to fall down. We went up in the elevator and got off on the fourteenth floor. That was where I learned that apartment buildings have no thirteenth floor. There were several apartments on that floor, and we went to his and rang the buzzer. I don't know why he didn't use a key. Maybe using the buzzer gave his wife a chance to cover up if she was nursing. She answered the door and he said, Marcia, this is Brighton. Brighton, Marcia. We nodded at each other. She was short and still fat from the baby. She looked worn out and at least in her thirties. She wore glasses and a floor-length nightgown, even though it was hot. It was very hot. As far as I could tell the apartment didn't even have a fan.

She led us back to see the baby who slept in the one bedroom with its parents. Her parents. I hate it when people call babies "it." Her name was Audrey. She was the ugliest baby I've ever seen. She had a lot of red birthmarks on her face, and her head was long and thin. I really thought something was wrong with her head. She was much too thin for a healthy baby, and one eye wouldn't open. Peter kept saying, look, she's winking, and Marcia, who I think knew better, said, she's not, Peter. She doesn't have that control yet. I said, I bet the light's in her eyes, and they agreed, yes, yes, and we left it at that. Also, I won't say much more about it but I know how babies smell. Even with something in their diaper they smell sweet. The top of their head smells of milk and powder. Audrey had a terrible smell. It was so sad I almost started to cry. She smelled metallic, like a train. Hot metal against hot metal. It made me think of the electric chair.

I was supposed to stay and eat with them but I pretended I'd forgotten about my sister's birthday. I said, we'll have to do it some other time. After that I didn't know what to do with Peter. I didn't know how to be with him. I thought a lot about children, and the mistakes parents make, and how you could never have a kid and expect your life to go on as it had before, as if nothing had happened. I realized this was true even if the kid died. I didn't know many adults without children. Everyone I worked with was married and had children, and you always knew more about the children than you did about the person they were married to. Susan, my boss, had three children, and she was only twenty-eight. She didn't go on and on about them at work like Peter did, but when they were new maybe she had. She had a photograph of them that took up the corner of her desk. Three boys, six, four and two years old, all in sailor suits. I wondered if Dad had a picture of us in his office. Next to that there was a tiny picture of her husband.

Dad, I was beginning to like. All summer we rode the train in together. Most of the time we just passed the newspaper back and forth and made small talk, but sometimes a real conversation happened. Once he said out of the blue, you know, I never liked the *Times*. It was always your mother's paper. I liked the *Tribune*.

So you guys got two papers? That's pretty fancy.

No. We got the *Times*.

That was more or less it for a while, then he said, it's a paper that takes itself too seriously.

I guess it does, I said.

The *Tribune* had funnies. I admire that in a first-class paper. I used to follow a comic strip called "Alley Oop." You don't remember Alley Oop?

I don't, Dad.

He was a caveman.

It's like pulling teeth sometimes with Dad. I said, well, what kind of stuff did he do?

Oh. Nothing memorable. I guess he did what they did back then, clubbed things, dragged ladies off by the hair.

That's it?

I don't think there was much more to it than that.

Huh, I said.

It's funny what you remember.

At the end of my job I was working with an author named Lee Samoset, who unfortunately no one's ever heard of, on a book called *Big Rigs 'n' Biscuits*. Dad was the one who came up with the title. We were going in on the train one day, talking about this book that was basically a guide to eating cheaply on the road, plus some philosophy thrown in, like *Zen and the Art of Motorcycle Maintenance,* but better. Lee Samoset is in spirit related to Will Rogers. He's pithy, which is a whole different branch of philosophy than what you get in *Zen.* Anyway, Dad said you need to put people at ease with a title. He suggested *Big Rigs 'n' Biscuits.* I said, but where's the philosophy? That covers the road and the food part of it, how about the philosophy? I forget he's a businessman. He said, the people you want to hit with this book are the people who travel. Anyone will buy a travel book. No one will buy a philosophy book. You figure your market first, then you sell to it. Never mind what the book's about. By the time they've bought it, it doesn't matter.

I was sort of blown away by that. I said, Dad, that's dishonest.

It's not dishonest. It's catering to the public.

No it's not. It's false advertising.

Listen, he said, people who buy something called a travel book will believe they're reading a travel book. That's human nature. You can't change human nature, you can only try and understand it. Those who understand it well do the best business. I don't think that's dishonest.

We had the courage to disagree. That was new for us. It gave us something to work with. I only mention this because not long after that conversation I made a choice that shattered Dad. Not a choice. I just enacted my destiny. I was happy then that we'd connected a little and did have something to work with. It meant he couldn't wring his hands forever, or wash his hands of me. Before that summer we could have said we'd never met, but by August we meant something to each other.

Big Rigs 'n' Biscuits never got through production. When I went off to NYU I left it in Peter's hands, where it stayed until the press folded. Dad asked about it all the time. I hated to tell him it wasn't ever coming out, so I lied. I lied until he stopped asking. I didn't think of it as being dishonest, I thought of it as understanding human nature and giving it no unnecessary disappointments.

Hal

Sooner or later they all fall across our doorstep. The halfway house for Haases, I call it. In fact, it's a modest, for me, apartment on Central Park West in the Seventies. We can walk to the opera in minutes. Brighton jogs in the park. We're right on the Macy's parade route. We have a guest room. I have a bedroom and a small study. Brighton has the maid's room, which he doesn't seem to mind. No bigger than a bread box, but with plenty of privacy. Our paths cross, when they cross, in the kitchen, or in the living room where he reads the paper with his feet up on the antiques. Behind him, facing the park, is the legendary window raked by Betty Boop's arm. This according to my pal Phillip, who used to live here.

We have Helen with us from San Francisco. A couple of days with her father in New Jersey, a couple of days here, then on to Vermont where Tommie's living with her women and goats. Back to the land, that's our squaw Tommie. This time it's a farm near Barre. I call it the lesbian theme park. No men allowed unless they're shlepping something, is my guess. Unless they've come to fix the hot water heater or help their mother move in. Which is what Brighton did. Mud season in Vermont, Tommie and her two suitcases. The call from Oregon — help me, Brighton — and off he went. Flew out, picked up the pieces and drove back with her, the boy who doesn't drive. He has an unhealthy patience for her whims. I know it well.

Helen I find hard to reach. She arrived last night and the three of us went out for Italian food, an unassuming place called La Bocca. I like their ossobuco. She's too thin, bordering on unattractive. She ate the parsley off the top of her primavera and left the rest. It doesn't take a genius to see what's happening, though Brighton doesn't see it. There's a family blindness involved. I lost a lot of weight myself once, but for good, healthy reasons. She's not dieting, she's caught. It starts as a need to control something in your life, then it becomes the next thing you lose your control to.

My friend Phillip did that to himself and almost died. It's not as common with men. We all watched him go down and didn't know how to help him, until he ended up in the hospital. Helen has already warned me with her eyes that it's none of my business, and let's please talk about someone else.

We stood outside La Bocca, waiting for Brighton who'd gone to the john. A balmy night. I love the end of September in New York. "How's your father?" I asked her.

"Oh, you know." She shrugged. "Dad and I don't really get along. He's a strange guy. I feel sorry for him."

"How long has it been since you saw him?"

"A long time."

"Do you think he's changed?"

"Not really."

"I do. I think he has."

She smiled, an unsettling smile, her trademark. "Then why ask me?"

The last time I saw Frank Haas was a chance meeting about a year ago in the gourmet section of Bloomingdale's. Frank grows more decent every day. He doesn't hold grudges. I've never believed him to be a complex man; nothing complicated about him. When I was younger I held this against him, Tommie and I both did. Now I find it a great relief. It makes him saintlike among vipers. He was fiddling with a state-of-the-art mixer. "Hello, Frank," I said. He gave me a warm hello back. He seemed more energetic than I'd ever seen him, a new lease on life. Suddenly I thought, my God, has he got a girlfriend? Maybe he's in love.

I was buying some knives, which he examined. "Is this a good kind to buy?" he asked. "I'm an idiot in the kitchen. We need some knives. These are French, aren't they? Sabatier. They must be."

"They hold an edge, that's why I buy them."

He lowered his voice conspiratorially. "Between you and me, I've never sharpened a knife in my life."

I laughed. "Well, sharpen the ones you've got first. That may be all they need, a little attention. I make kitchen decisions impulsively, but it's not the best way."

"Oh, I never do."

He was wearing a gray business suit and a forest green tie with a pattern of oak leaves and acorns on it. Probably a squirrel or two, I didn't look that closely. I made a mental note: Christmas present for Frank, solid color silk ties. He still worked at Channel 13 after all these years. That was just like him, the steady, measured approach to whatever he did, like a long-distance walker. He asked me how my work was going.

"You knew I left Saks?"

"That's what Brighton said."

"I was at a dead end there."

He nodded. "Now you're selling antiques? Is that what it is?"

"Buying. My partner does the selling. Retail doesn't much interest me."

"Well, I think that's great."

Frank is a shy man. After all these years I suddenly saw it. The stubborn bulldog streak had gone away. I pointed to his mixer. It was really quite a gadget. "Is that for you, or a gift?" I fully expected him to mention a lady friend.

"It's a gift for me."

"Really?"

He sighed. "It's a possible gift for me. It would be so useful."

"What does it do?"

"Just about anything. What I like is the bread hook." He showed me the bread hook. "You can mix up anything in here. Cakes, breads, yeast breads. It comes highly recommended by my son."

"That's worth something," I said.

Frank nodded. "He gave me all the information about it except the price." He showed me the price tag. "A little steep. What do you think?"

"Steep," I agreed, "but this is Bloomy's."

"I don't know where else to go."

"Anywhere. I have a catalog place, they'll have it for half that."

I promised him the address. He thanked me. We said goodbye and went our ways. That night I was about to tell Brighton the story, then thought not to. The vision of Frank Haas navigating the culinary aspects of life solo, with only the casual advice of his son, saddened me. It made my face long. But maybe I was wrong. I asked Brighton, "You don't think your father has a new woman friend, do you?"

"He didn't yesterday. You mean like a girlfriend?"

I nodded.

"No. No way. He'd tell me."

"I don't know why he'd tell you. Not right away. Wouldn't he feel guilty? He's still a married man."

"I think he'll always be married to Mom. It's sad, but I don't think he's ever going to fall in love with someone else."

I do, but I didn't say it. Hope springs eternal, like it or not. It's been a year since then. While there's no actual sign of a woman in his life, there are signs aplenty that he's joining the human race. He's still Frank Haas, but he's reaching out to his son for a change, and vice versa. I suspect from Helen's visit that a similar process is happening with his daughter. I wish him all the luck in the world with that one.

We had breakfast together this morning, which meant Helen sat and sipped black coffee and watched her brother and me eat. I find it maddening to be watched by those insatiable eyes that pretend they need nothing. Only the wounded can appear so righteous. Am I a glutton for my two poached eggs and English muffin? That second cup of coffee? I feel like shaking her. I've asked Brighton not to go to work today, not to leave her alone here. What am I afraid of, that she'll rifle through my drawers and slash my shirts? Ax the antiques? No. Do herself harm.

He left first. She sat in front of the window reading the paper. I got up and poured myself another, a third, cup of coffee. "You know about that window behind you?" I said.

"What window?"

"The one behind you."

"What about it?"

"Your brother didn't tell you?"

She dropped the paper and sighed. "No. What about it?"

"Betty Boop hit it."

"Betty Boop?"

"You know who that is."

"Of course I know who that is."

"She ploughed right into it."

"Excuse me?"

"I wasn't here. My friend Phillip lived here then."

"Speak English, Hal."

"Betty Boop. The balloon in the Macy's parade. I guess it was windy and she crashed into the window."

"She broke it?"

"No, I don't think so."

"Then what was the big deal?"

I shrugged. "Hard to describe. I guess you had to be there." Most people go ga-ga when I tell them that story. Understand, Hal, I said to myself, who you're dealing with here is not most people.

She went back to her paper and I finished my coffee. I left the room to shave and came back, ready for work, which these days means blue jeans and an old Oxford shirt, usually pink, no tie, and a cardigan. Brighton calls this my release from the fashion industry. Helen looked at me. "That's how you go to work?"

"Sure."

"You're kidding."

I laughed. "The antiques don't care."

"I'd give anything to go to work like that."

"What do you wear?"

"Well, different things."

"On an average day what would it look like? A dress?"

"No. A skirt. Sometimes a suit."

"I bet you look good."

"Not really. I look like everyone else."

"Everyone else doesn't have your height. Or your face. You've got a model's face."

"It's Tommie's face."

"Yes, it is."

"Those guys wore the strangest clothes, didn't they?"

"Your mother's what I call an idiosyncratic dresser."

"I think Dad's color blind."

"You know how to tell?"

"Look at what he wears. He's Mr. Goofball."

"The test is if his socks don't match."

"Nothing matches. I wonder if people make fun of him behind his back. I mean at work."

"I don't think it would ruffle Frank."

"I do."

She was wearing a pair of old gray sweatpants I coveted, and a newer, baggy gray sweatshirt. Gray was not her color, not at this time in her life. Maybe with a little more flesh and ruddiness to her, though the Haases weren't known for ruddiness. "I can think of some casual clothes, some comfortable clothes you'd look terrific in, Helen. Like silk pants. You'd look great in silk."

"It's dressy."

"It doesn't have to be. You could wear it to work and be plenty fancy, but comfortable."

"That's what I'm looking for. People are so into image, even out there. This place I work, the Mead Foundation, you'd think it would be the most relaxed place in the world, just a bunch of nerdy anthropologists grubbing for money."

"Those places can't afford not to keep up an image. They're begging, and beggars are unfortunately judged by their appearance."

"Even out there."

"Everywhere."

"Nobody understands the West Coast, Hal. At least not the Bay area. Haight Ashbury is all they think of."

"And gays."

"Yeah. Gays."

We were quiet for a minute, quiet and somewhat peaceful, at least I was. Finally she said, "I'm really nervous about seeing Tommie."

"I bet you are."

"I don't want it to happen again. I couldn't stand that. You know what I mean?"

"I don't really know what happened between you two."

"You don't?"

"How could I? You weren't talking."

"No, I wasn't."

"You weren't talking, and then you left home."

"That was smart."

"Everything you've done has been smart, Helen. Going away, staying away, coming back. That's all smart."

"Not everything's been smart. I'm afraid of people right now. I don't know how to be with them. That's not so smart. And I'm kind of too thin."

"Yes, you are."

"It's not full-blown, Hal. I know what you're thinking."

"I'm not thinking anything."

"You are. But it's not that. It's hard for me to eat in front of other people, that's all. When you leave I'll have breakfast, I'll make myself a couple of eggs or something. I'm not much of a cook."

"You're pretty, Helen."

"Well. I don't know."

"You'd be prettier if you weighed more."

"I think I need to get Tommie out of the way first."

"Can I tell you something?"

"Is it advice? I don't want advice."

"Don't wait for Tommie."

"That's advice."

"Then ignore it. I love Tommie but she's not worth giving your life to. Nobody is."

"That's pretty cynical."

"Why?"

"You should know why. I thought giving your life was the point."

"Not giving it away."

She shook her head. "I don't understand relationships."

"I don't either."

"Yes, you do. You've lived with people. You were married, remember?"

I laughed. "I vaguely remember. It was a flop. They've all been flops."

"Not Brighton."

"No. But he's not in my bed."

"He never was?"

"No. Oh, no."

"I thought he was."

Sobering thought.

Before I left I made sure she knew where the frying pan was. I pulled out bacon and eggs and orange juice, and what was left of Brighton's homemade bread. All day at work I thought about how she had, that morning, stepped forward into the path of an oncoming unknown — me. She had made the brave move, and in two days time she would make it again with Tommie. She was on her way. Not literally — she was sitting at my table, I hoped, reacquainting herself with food and nourishment, which is what I could offer her now, a stocked kitchen. But she was launched, she was moving. Towards life, is what I felt.

I felt surprisingly tender towards her willingness to hear who had or hadn't been in my bed. She was full of doubt, Helen. She didn't trust the ground she walked on, and why should she? I guessed what had happened between her and Tommie was similar to what had always been between me and my own mother — the feeling that when they died, it would be we who killed them. A strange conviction. In Helen's case, I could see her solution had been to die first.

Brighton

One of the things Hal and I had to get used to was being right up against each other's private lives. He was seeing someone, a man named Charles who worked for the Metropolitan Museum. He was a lawyer. He was Hal's age or a little older. He wore pin-striped suits and bow ties, shirts with cufflinks, expensive looking loafers. He carried an attaché case and a hundred-and-sixty-dollar umbrella, but I liked him. He was something new for Hal. He didn't need to be taken care of. The first time I met him was at the apartment when he came over to have dinner with us. It was a Friday night and he came in the door with a bouquet of white roses. You're Brighton, he said. I was sitting on the sofa and he came over and shook my hand. Hal came out of the kitchen and Charles kissed him in front of me.

Hal looked embarrassed and I said, I'll get you a vase for those. I got up and went into the kitchen to give them some privacy, but Hal came bustling in after me. I said, I'll get it. Go back out to your friend.

Charles liked everything Hal cooked that night and he said so more than once. He was almost a dapper man. I could imagine him in a top hat with a silver-studded cane. He had short, dark hair, neatly trimmed, almost impeccably trimmed. If he had a flaw, that was it: too impeccable. He spent almost as much time talking to me as he did to Hal, if not more. Hal kept getting up and doing things in the kitchen, to give us time to get to know each other I guess. Finally at about eleven o'clock the meal was over and I said, so what are you two up to tonight? Are you going out?

Are we? said Charles, raising his eyebrows at Hal. Hal didn't look very happy.

I thought I knew what the problem was and I said, I've got some plans for the evening. I should probably get going right now, in fact. I got up and took a few dishes out to the kitchen, then went to my room and got some money and my coat. When I came back to say good-bye, Charles had moved his chair closer to Hal's and Hal stood up quickly and said, listen, uh, Brighton. He sort of laughed.

It's fine, I said. I'm supposed to meet somebody. I better hustle. Nice meeting you, I said to Charles. Come back any time.

He gave a little wave and said, don't stay out too late now, and laughed. Hal, all through this, looked slightly mortified.

What I did that night was walk down to Washington Square Park and back. On the way home I stopped for ice cream in an all-night Czech coffee shop. I had no one to meet. Who would I be meeting at eleven o'clock at night? I didn't have night friends. I liked walking alone in the dark, or as dark as it got in New York. Things didn't slow down at night. What happened was the day crowd folded up and the night crowd got going.

Even little kids were out on the street, all jazzed up, climbing in and out of their strollers.

Hal slept late the next morning. I made some coffee for myself and when I heard him in the bathroom I made a cup for him. He came out. I said, there's your coffee.

Oh. Thanks.

I just made it.

That was nice of you.

I like the smell of it twice in the morning.

Good. Yeah, I do too.

He came and sat down and I said, so Charles didn't spend the night? Hal didn't say anything. I said, I like him.

Yeah?

He's a good choice for you. He's more like you than Jody was. You can have a conversation with him.

That's true.

He sipped his coffee and looked around for the paper. I said, I think he might like you more than you like him.

Charles?

I could be wrong. Maybe it's not a problem. You just seemed a little cool to him, that's all.

Huh.

I'm probably wrong.

No. I wouldn't say you're wrong.

Well, if you don't want to talk about it, that's fine. I just ask because if this person's not going to be in your life a whole lot longer, I don't want to, you know, get used to him.

That makes sense.

What's your take on it? Just so I know.

What's my take on it? The paper was on the chair next to him and he put it on the table.

Maybe this isn't a conversation we need to have.

No, we do. We do, he said. I just don't know how to have it. I'll tell you something, Brighton, this is new territory for me. I've never been around anyone who talked before. Not men.

I think he's good for you that way.

I'm talking about you.

Me? I said.

You're the communicator. Who would have thought that? You were a very closed-mouth kid.

I remember opening my mouth.

To bite me.

Well, maybe you deserved it.

That interested him. How?

I don't know. Everybody had to like you, that was your rule. I thought it was a stupid rule. I hardly knew you.

He was quiet a minute. He said, I think it's still my rule.

I can understand that, but it's sad. Here comes Charles, somebody who likes you a lot but has his own life and doesn't depend on you, and what's your reaction? Not too interested. I think your new rule is that everybody has to need you. He looked at me in a kind of panic and I said, I'm not trying to lay anything on you. I'm just trying to keep the channels open. We're just having a conversation. It's okay.

The amazing thing was he started to cry. We sat there at the table with our coffee and the paper and last night's tablecloth showing a few wine stains. It's okay, I said a couple more times. Finally he must have really believed it was okay, and would be okay, because he said, the two people I've loved most in my life are my mother and your mother. That's the truth, Brighton. Men have always been from the neck down only. Someone like Charles, I don't know what to do with. I don't know where he fits. He doesn't. He doesn't fit. I look at you with him, relating to him like he's a person, a full person, and I think what's the matter with you, Hal? I feel ashamed. You have no idea how ashamed I feel, how cut off I feel, how cut in two. Hal Chapin the son and Hal Chapin the lover. They've never met. Sex is a dirty little secret. It's a thrill. If it's not a thrill it's over. He shifted in his chair. Charles and I have been seeing each other for about eight weeks. I like him. I like him very much. Our time in bed is not thrilling. It was, but now it's not. At least for me it's not. This makes me sad because I like his company very much.

I hadn't expected all that. Hal said, what would you do?

What do you mean, do?

He laughed. I guess that's the answer right there.

I don't know much about this stuff, I said. People stuff. Hardly anything. If I had someone I liked I'd hold on to them. I hope I would. It's easy to say. I've never had anyone I liked like that.

Something happened to you kids, said Hal. You and Helen. You're just not in a hurry, either of you.

You mean, like what?

Like girlfriends, boyfriends, dating. All that crap that teenagers do. I don't know how you got around it. I only got around it because I was locked up with boys in a boarding school. My first heaven and hell.

You met Mom, I said.

Not until college.

Did you date Mom?

Sure.

You did?

Of course I did. We double-dated. She and Jeanne Ann and Bobby Kahn and I.

In what configuration? He laughed, and I said, did you ever sleep with Mom?

He looked at me. You ask her that.

I did.

What was her answer?

She said yes, but ask Hal.

Yes is my answer too.

It was true, until college I didn't know what a date was. Or I should say, I knew enough to steer clear of that particular form of involvement. Going to bed with people I somewhat understood, but dating, going on a date, sitting through a movie with someone you hardly knew, aware of your sweaty palms and metal breath — it seemed like nothing but a bad time. Helen and I were both very socially awkward when it came to the opposite sex. I don't know why this happens in a family. We were spared, that's how I look at it. I had feelings, plenty of feelings, like lust and stuff, but that was such a private part of my life I never would have thought of sharing it with anyone. Not for a long time.

I understood what Hal meant about being cut in two because I felt it myself. He was farther along with it, and he'd grown up in a less free time, a less tolerant time, but I knew what he was talking about. I hadn't articulated it to myself. I didn't talk to myself about my body hardly at all. I was a little afraid to.

One thing I did, I was starting to do, was run. For exercise. I'd jog in the park every morning and then I'd walk down to NYU. I was starting to walk everywhere. On the weekends I'd walk out to Brooklyn and back. I liked Brooklyn. I liked the low buildings. It was like walking to Europe. My legs were getting strong, I could feel the difference in what they could tolerate. It was nice to get into bed at night and instead of just going to sleep, actually touching my legs. They were a pretty solid unit. I started to notice that my arms were sort of squooshy, so I did a regular routine of push-ups every morning before the run. I hate push-ups. I hate that kind of fake exercise. But how else was I going to get the arms in there? I asked Hal what he thought and he said, you should swim. I said, water doesn't thrill me. Then stick to your push-ups, he said. Or just be flabby like me. He isn't flabby but he doesn't exercise.

The weather got colder. Some mornings I didn't feel like jogging against that cold wind. If I didn't jog I didn't feel good about myself. I decided to join the West Sixty-third Street Y. They had an indoor track and a weight room, and some tennis courts and squash courts. They had a pool. The guy who was showing me around said, you gotta see the pool. He was a real New Yorker, that guy. I said, no thanks, I don't swim. Aw, come on, he said, this pool is something else. He took me in, you went in through the locker room, and there was the pool. I'd never seen an indoor pool before. It had lights in the bottom of it. There wasn't one person in it. The lights came up through the blue water and made a picture I would have liked to paint if I was a painter. The surface wasn't still, it kind of breathed. The tiles were white. It looked like it had been newly tiled, and there were a few potted plants around. Somewhere deep in the building you could hear a pump working. It was quiet in there. Sometimes a little water sloshed into the gutter. I said, you swim?

Nah. I just take my lunch breaks in here.

Does the smell bother you? The chlorine?

Nah. I like it.

I kind of do too.

It's all new, he said. Old, but done up new. You should've seen it before. Tiles falling off, things floating in the water. No one came in here.

People use it now?

Oh, sure. This just happens to be off-hours. The lunch hour's busy, and six to seven-thirty in the a.m. You wouldn't get me up that early to get in the water. I don't like getting wet. I eat my lunch here.

My hair was long then, and the first thing I was told was I'd have to wear a bathing cap. That or cut it. I cut it. Suddenly I had my neck back again, my neck and my face. If you're ever feeling at a crossroads, try cutting your hair. One day after jogging on the indoor track I went in and looked at the pool. I stood by it, getting used to the idea of it. It had been a long time since I'd been in the water. Even in the summer if I was hot I'd just get in the shower. That day there were a couple of people swimming, an old man and an old woman who might have been married. She was a breaststroker, probably to keep her hair dry, even though she was wearing a cap. He did the sidestroke and the backstroke. She saw me and waved and said, come on in, it's just us chickens. I said, I'm thinking about it. She said, don't think, thinking's dangerous. She laughed and plopped forward into her breaststroke and I went into the locker room and came out wearing my bathing suit which was actually an old plaid one of Dad's.

Her name was Bridget and in a way I can't describe she reminded me of Mrs. DiAngelo. The man swimming next to her was her brother, not her husband. She told me he was a retired New York City cop. I sat on the edge of the pool with my legs in the water. Bridget would do a lap, then rest, another lap, then rest. Every time she rested she'd talk to me or to her brother or to both of us. She told me about a sweater she was knitting for her niece.

That was the first time, and I only got my legs wet. After that it was easy. I began to swim regularly, every morning before my ten o'clock class. I'd run down to the Y, hop in the pool, swim half a mile without stopping, get out, get in the shower, get dressed and walk down to NYU. I saw less and less of Hal. We saw each other on weekends unless he went out to visit his mother in Connecticut. On those weekends I had the apartment to myself and sometimes I'd have my friend Roger over. He was a friend from school and he lived in a real dump, a tiny apartment he shared with a couple who fought like cats and dogs. I'd have him over and he'd sleep in the guest room and we'd eat meals together and walk, usually out to Prospect Park in Brooklyn, or up to Harlem. He'd spend the whole weekend. I'd never had a friend like that, not even Maria. Sometimes we'd look through *The New Yorker* and pick out five things to do on a Saturday and go do them. Or do one of them. We always had great intentions culture-wise.

One weekend I took him to the Y as my guest. We jogged on the track, then we rented some racquets and played squash. Roger knew how to play because even though his family wasn't rich he'd been to a prep school. He told me the last time he'd been in a squash court was when he was tripping on acid.

He's about my height. At that time he weighed a little more than me. His hair is light brown and full of cowlicks when it's short. He wanted to be a high-school teacher, and in fact that's what he did become. I see him whenever I'm out in San Francisco, which is where he lives with his wife Connie. Of the two of us, he was always the leader. He'd lived in Japan, he'd been kicked out of school, he had three older brothers, his parents were divorced. He was more carefree than me. Also more careless. Walking up to Harlem was his idea, I never would have thought of it. We even went to the movies up there and walked back to Hal's apartment in the dark. A few times we smoked pot in the apartment.

Even though they'd never met, Roger knew Hal was gay. I didn't tell him, he just knew. He said, what's that like? I was lying on the sofa after dinner. We'd had steak and ice cream. I said, what do you mean?

To hang out with, like, gays?

I don't hang out with gays.

You live with this guy. He must bring his friends over.

Not really. No. Sometimes his boyfriend is here but that's all. I've known him since I was a kid, so I'm used to it.

You always knew he was gay?

He wasn't. He was married.

That doesn't mean anything.

Well, I don't think he knew.

He knew, said Roger.

Then why did he get married?

To prove he wasn't gay.

He came over and sat on the floor next to me while he rolled a joint. I got up and opened the window. I didn't like the smell of pot in Hal's apartment.

It's your apartment too, said Roger.

I guess.

You live here. You pay rent here. He passed me the joint. You entertain here.

I laughed. I didn't know what to do but laugh. It was strong pot. We sat on the sofa for a while, saying nothing. I put my head back and closed my eyes and when I opened them again Roger was looking at me very intently. I'm interested in you, he said. I nodded and closed my eyes again. We sat for a long time, then he got up and went into the guest room and got ready for bed. I could hear him taking off his blue jeans, the sound of the cloth, heavy and slurred. The bed creaked when he got in it. It was a soft, uncomfortable bed. I heard him put his watch on the night table, and I heard his body turn over.

We started a regular weekend routine of working out together at the Y. Squash, jogging and weight room. Sometimes we'd shoot baskets in the gym. More and more we'd use the pool. Roger was an easy swimmer. He taught me how to do flipturns. Afterwards we'd sit in the steam room and watch the bodies, each one letting in a puff of cool air as the door opened and closed. The foggy bodies. Then we'd shower and go out for something to eat, or if Hal was gone we'd go home and I'd make something.

I was learning how to cook. Hal was a good cook, lots of butter, and the little time we spent together we spent in the kitchen. I always thought Mom could cook, because she got a hot meal on the table most of the time and it was usually edible. By the time I left home we were living on spaghetti. Dad could boil water, I could make a pretty good tomato sauce out of a can. Helen didn't eat with us much at that time. I don't know where she ate.

I like cooking for people. It gives you time to catch up with yourself, to have a conversation with yourself. I would probably like knitting too. Roger sat in the living room listening to Hal's records, or reading, or watching TV, while I worked in the kitchen. Sometimes he'd come in and say, what's cooking? Sometimes he'd come up behind me and look over my shoulder, or put his chin on my shoulder. He smelled of chlorine, we both did. After working out, my body felt calm and full of energy. I was really liking it, liking the feeling that swimming gave me. We were regular swimmers now.

One weekend when Hal was away, on a Sunday, we wanted to work out early. I went into Roger's room with a cup of coffee to wake him up. He slept in his underwear and T-shirt. I put the coffee on the night table. Thanks, he said. I said, spinach and feta cheese omelet when you get up. We ate and went down to the Y and did a light workout in the weight room, feeling a little sluggish from breakfast. The pool wasn't open yet but we wanted to swim. We changed into our suits. No one was in the locker room. It was still pretty early. We went through to the pool and no one had turned the lights on yet. A few high windows kept it from being completely dark. It was shadowy, suspenseful. Roger got in the water first. We didn't talk, we didn't even whisper. He swam underwater to the other end of the pool. I watched him disappear and come up again, then I got in.

He came back to my end of the pool and stood next to me. Then he sort of ducked under and came up with a wad of something in his hand. He put it on the side of the pool. It was his bathing suit. He swam away again and I took mine off and went underwater and kicked off. It felt great. The naked part felt unbelievably great. I didn't think about what would happen if the lights went on, I didn't think about anything. I remembered what Bridget had said and I took her advice.

After about five minutes Roger came up to me in the shallow end and did something very simple. He put his hands on my shoulders and put his lips on my mouth. He didn't really kiss me. Then he turned me around so I was facing the side of the pool and he was facing my back. I didn't think, I just went where he moved me. He pressed against me and put his arms around my waist and his hands down in my hair. I said, I like what's happening, I just don't like it happening here. The guy could come in.

He's not coming in, said Roger.

He might. I don't want to be here when he does.

We put our suits on and went back into the locker room and got dressed and went home. I went into my room and took my clothes off and lay down on my bed. He came in a minute later and closed the door. I said, excuse the sheets. They're kind of ripe.

This room is all bed.

I know.

He undressed and came down next to me. He put his hand on my chest. I'm shaking, he said.

I know it.

I'm shaking all over.

I know.

I found his leg and rubbed against it and he smiled.

I don't know what I thought sex would be like. Anatomically there were some things I couldn't imagine. He brought his mouth down to mine and bit me hard on the lip, which surprised me. That's when I knew in my body that pain was part of this, and if it was any good it would always be.

Hal

As for Tommie, our last encounter was not a happy one. She came down this past Fourth of July to spend a few days with us in Connecticut. My mother, Brighton and me. Add Tommie to that and you have a foolproof recipe for fireworks. She drove down on the day itself. Our plan was to get through that day, wake up and get through the next one. Lots of conversation, cool drinks, good food. The morning before she arrived I locked myself in the kitchen and brought all my concentration to bear on a Portuguese dish called *bacalhau*. Normally I don't do Portuguese, but Phillip had made this for us once and it was exquisite. Delicate if done right, with just the right amount of garlic and oil. If done wrong, go directly to jail, do not pass go.

Why I chose to add risk to risk that weekend, I can't imagine. I had seen Tommie only a few times, briefly, since she moved back east. Twice Brighton and I went up to Vermont to spend an afternoon with her, and once, on her way to New Jersey, she stopped in the city for lunch. This was scheduled to be her longest visit. It was certainly the hottest. Noon broke ninety-five. Horrible humidity. A house full of jerry-rigged fans. Brighton sat in front of the television in the living room, watching junk. The shades were pulled against the heat and it gave the room a cave-like look and the feel of a household in mourning.

I was at the end of the *bacalhau* when he came into the kitchen. "You look troubled," I said. He looked unhappy and young.

"That's a dumb thing to say. What are you making?"

"It's called *bacalhau*."

"What is it?"

"Basically, a codfish pâté."

"Do you want me to cook tonight?"

"I thought we'd have this."

"Oh. Okay. It looked more like a lunch thing. Do you know when she's coming?"

"My guess is about four or five, depending on traffic."

"Do you think we'll last three days in this house together?"

"I don't know. What's your bet?"

"I bet we won't."

"I guess I'll have to bet we will, just to have a bet."

"You can bet what I bet."

"That's not a bet."

"If it's what you believe, who cares what it is."

He sat down at the kitchen table, his elbow next to a jar of peanuts. I knew within a minute he'd open the jar and pour some peanuts into his hand, lean his head back and drop them one by one into his mouth. Within a minute he did.

I like working in my mother's kitchen. She was a wonderful cook. After my father left, she had different boyfriends who could cook. I don't remember them, I only remember a later boyfriend named Martin. One of the boyfriends was French, I'm guessing, because French is what Jane did best. I remember going to school with leftover coq au vin in my lunchbox. By the time I was nine I could make a foolproof omelette — and spelled it that way. Two beaten eggs, fresh herbs, a splash of water not milk, the right pan at the right heat, the omelette forming only the thinnest skin between what it contained and the world. A capful of vinegar thrown in the hot pan at the end, then dribbled over the omelette to clean the palate. The French are fanatic about cleaning the palate. We ate salad only at the end of a meal, and never dressed it until immediately before we ate it. There was always a Brie or Camembert ripening somewhere in the house, and loaves of crusty French bread. My favorite breakfast was Camembert and mustard on crackers. Coq au vin for lunch. Omelettes for supper with French bread dipped in wine or coffee. Jane made wonderful coffee.

Brighton grew up on tuna fish casserole. Tuna fish casserole and an occasional fallen soufflé. In his family, the entrée was nothing but the necessary path to dessert. It's a wonder those kids weren't blimps. The first fancy dish he ever made for me was baked Alaska. Ice cream in the oven, the great American anomaly. Like Ritz cracker apple-less apple pie. Out of respect for his enthusiasm and potential, I ate what was put in front of me. It was unbearably sweet, the meringue too tough, reminding me of the cups of women's bathing suits. The next day I taught him how to make flan, which satisfies his need for sweet and mine for rich and eggy.

Tommie arrived in the evening, around six o'clock. I was bathing my mother, getting her ready for her night, which starts early. The bath is our ritual. I like it and I'm possessive about it.

In the heat it helps her sleep, a cool bath before bed. I run water in the tub and carry her in and sit her up. Until you've bathed someone, someone of weight who leans on you, you never realize how hard a bathroom is. It's made of cold, hard, unwelcoming materials. Kneeling on the floor by a tub is painful. Sitting in a bathtub is painful. A coffin is more comfortable. Jane has a wonderful old claw-and-ball bathtub, visually soothing but very hard on her bones. My job has been to soften her environment. After her last stroke I bought her some good thick towels and thick rugs for the bathroom floor. I found something that looks like a weighted air mattress that fits inside the bathtub. She has her sea sponges and her different soaps. Rose and cucumber she likes the best. Sometimes she likes a bubble bath.

I heard the car drive up as I was soaping her back, then an unexpected sound — a dog barking. It sounded like a good-sized dog, and I wondered if Tommie could possibly have been so gauche as to bring a dog with her. I don't like dogs. They poop on my lawn. Jane looked worried. I said, "Tommie's here. I don't know who the dog belongs to." I wondered if she'd remember Tommie. I hoped she would. My instinct was that it would be easier for all of us if she did. I'd let Brighton handle it.

I finished washing her. I lifted her out and took her over to what she calls her divan at the foot of her bed. I laid her down on it and powdered her and put her diaper on for the night. I put a clean nightgown on her and put her to bed. I was in no hurry. This was the time of day when I felt closest to her. Physically, we had never been closer. There was always that point when I started to sponge her down, her back first, then her flattened breasts, when a wave of confusion and shame came over me. Shame is too strong a word. An awakened taboo. If she felt something similar, she gave no sign of it. Her skin came alive under the sponge. She seemed to like it and relax under it.

"Goodnight, Mom," I said. We held hands for a minute. "I'll send Brighton in to say goodnight in a little while."

I walked through the house, towards the hum of voices. Brighton and Tommie were sitting on the porch, watching her great big dog do its business on the lawn. Tommie was wearing a yellow sundress, something only she can pull off, pun intended, at age fifty, and a floppy cotton hat and espadrilles. She looked like a Wellesley girl on her junior year abroad and I told her so. I also told her to get that animal on a leash.

"He's always so happy to see me," she said to Brighton. "Is he always so happy to see you?" She got up and went across the lawn to the car, calling the lummox after her. She came back with several yards of clothesline, one end of which she tied to his collar. He sat at her feet, his tongue dripping in the heat. I realized he was an old dog, even a very old dog, whose interest in doing me harm, or harm to the property, was zero. Dogs have to poop, so he pooped on the lawn. Where else? Drop it, Hal, I thought.

I sat down in a chair. "What's his name?" I asked.

Tommie leaned over and said to the dog, "He's trying to make it up to us."

"That's Penelope," said Brighton.

I looked at him. "The dog's name's Penelope?"

"Yeah. It's a she."

"She's an old she," I said.

"How old is she, Mom?"

"No idea."

"She's part Alsatian," said Brighton. "Definitely."

"She's got a sweet head," I said.

"He's trying to work his way back in," Tommie said to the dog. "Do we let him?"

"How was your trip?" I asked.

She flattened the dog's ears, something it seemed to like. "She's not so sure about you."

"I bet it was hot," I said.

"Hot?" She laughed.

"How was the traffic?"

"Awful. Penelope slept the whole way."

I smiled. "It's not going to be easy for me to call her Penelope. I'll tell you why sometime."

"You don't have to call her anything. Just be nice to her. She's an old dog."

"I guess she doesn't need to be on the leash. Sorry, Penelope. Human foibles." The dog looked up at me. They can look more human than humans sometimes, another thing I hold against them. "Will you explain that to her?"

"You explain it," said Tommie. "They're your foibles."

"I will," said Brighton. He got down on all fours next to the dog. Her tongue came up and covered his mouth and he laughed. He lay down next to her on the porch boards and slung his arm over her back. Sometimes, around Tommie, I feel like he's our son and it embarrasses me. He whispered something to the dog, who yawned and threw her tongue around some more. "Got that?" he said. He shook her paw and stood up and went back to his chair.

Tommie was watching me watch him. "A dog would do you good, Hal."

"In the city?"

"The city's full of dogs."

"Remember Snakie?" said Brighton.

She laughed. "What was the minister's name?"

"It was the cab driver who had the name."

"What was his name?"

"I forget. I remember we got in the cab and he said, 'That's not a dog you got,' and you said, 'Certainly not, it's a snake. It won't hurt you. It's had its teeth out.' "

Tommie smiled. "What was the minister's great line?"

"It was your line, Mom. His wife asked if Snakie liked kids, and Helen said, 'We think so, but it didn't like me or my brother, that's why we're getting rid of it.' His wife said, 'Oh, that couldn't be true,' and you said, 'It's true, she wouldn't lie. My children don't have much natural affection, at least my son has none, and this was his dog.' "

"I said that?"

"Well, it was sort of true, I think."

"It was a terrible thing to say. Why do you remember it?"

"It was no big deal, Mom. It was part of the Snakie story. That was our best story."

"Well, I don't like it," she said. "It makes me feel very depressed."

I went in and brought out some ice water. I heard them talking about Helen. Tommie was saying, "You were just out there. Does she need a rug?" She glanced up at me as I handed her a glass. "Thank you," she said, without a drop of thanks in it.

A decade ago we went to war with each other over the fact that she fashioned herself as my conscience. Corrupting minors, was her accusation. More specifically, stealing her son. Almost overnight she became chaotic, though the seeds of it were sown in Providence, Rhode Island, where we first met. Her personal chaos has stood in the way of many things, communication for one, happiness for another. I don't see her at a dead end. If anything, I see her in a life that moves too fast, that keeps her moving and juggling and running. Seizures are the most likely disorder for her. I think her mind and body crave those fertile minutes of blackout when she can rest and not remember. I love Tommie. To come so far and be estranged, or even cautious, saddens me. Every time I see her, I expect we'll make our peace, though I no longer envision a moment, a flash of unity. I see it as a slow laying down of hostilities, from which, not a phoenix, but something more like a mayfly, rises. I don't think either of us expected our lives to include each other in exactly these ways.

"Well, I'm going back to the tube," said Brighton. He stretched and looked at his watch. "In five minutes."

"He's addicted to junk," I said.

"No, he's not," said Tommie. "He's escaping. I wish you liked baseball, Brighton."

"Why? I like it."

"Then we wouldn't have to fight over the TV."

"There's a game on?"

"It's summer, dodo. There's always a game on. It's a double-header. It might be over now. They were in extra innings. I listened to most of it in the car."

"We can watch it," said Brighton. "Let's go watch it with Jane. She has a little TV in her room. She likes baseball."

I laughed.

"She does, Hal. She'd like to see you, Mom."

"Jane? She won't remember me."

"She might."

"I haven't seen her in, what? More than twenty years."

"Well, she might," said Brighton.

"Where is she?" asked Tommie.

"She's in bed," I said.

"Oh. This early? Do we want to wake her up? It's just base-ball."

"She never really goes to sleep until I go in and say goodnight to her," said Brighton.

"I don't want to confuse her," said Tommie.

"You won't. She'll remember you, Mom."

I put together a plate of whipped cream cheese on melba toast and sent the two of them in. Often, after a snack, she was more alert. I stayed in the kitchen getting supper together. A minute later Brighton came in, fanning his nose. "A diaper not to be believed," he said.

"Oh, God. Let me change her."

"I'll do it, but I think we're out of diapers."

"We can't be."

"I didn't see any in there."

"Try next to the washing machine. There should be a whole box."

He came back with a stack of diapers. "What did she eat for lunch?" he asked.

"Some soup and some of your flan."

"That's all?"

"No. Guess."

"Codfish pâté?"

I laughed. "She was a test case."

He rolled his eyes. "This is going to be a fun house tomorrow morning."

"It's a fun house now, isn't it?"

He looked at me soberly. "She's so mean to you, Hal."

"She is mean."

"I remember when she wasn't."

"Good. Remember that."

"Well, I better get back in there."

"I can do it if you don't want to."

"I don't mind doing it."

"I don't either."

"It's just shit."

I threw a loaf of French bread in the oven, made a salad and set the table. I knew Tommie's taste ran to Mozart, and I put on *The Marriage of Figaro*. Not a personal favorite by any means, but I was actively working for peace in that house. I went out on the porch and sat down. I'd forgotten about the dog, Penelope, so soundly asleep I was worried she might be dead. She was breathing. I went inside and brought out a bowl of water and put it by her nose and wondered why we hadn't thought of this before, why someone hadn't. Dogs always need water after long car trips, that's what I remembered. Especially in that heat. For a short time we had two Dalmatians. One belonged to Thomas, the other to Louise. When I was of dog-owning age I was given my choice: a dachshund or piano lessons. Dachshunds weren't a kid's dog. On our block there was a pair that wore red sweaters all winter, and in the rain, little rain boots. They were walked by a black maid. They looked like a couple of miniature horses wearing saddle blankets. I said thank you, I'll take the piano lessons.

Tommie came out and found me. "I gave your dog some water," I said. She didn't say anything. "Did Jane fall asleep on you?"

"No, she didn't fall asleep on me."

"Sometimes she does."

"Well, she didn't. Do we have to have this music?"

"It's Mozart."

"It's deafening."

"I'll go turn it down," I said. "Or off. How about off?" She didn't respond and I said, "Off it is."

I came back out and sat down. I could see a storm brewing, but stupidly I plowed ahead. The truth is, I have always been a little afraid of Tommie in a dark mood, and my human instinct is to pretend the sun is shining when it's not. I said, "How's the baseball?"

"Why didn't you tell me she was dying? She's sitting there waiting to die, it's horrible. She can't even move."

"She can move. She can move her left arm. And her bowels, apparently. She's good at that. What more does she need?"

"Be serious."

"I'm dead serious. She can eat and shit, that's twice what your dog can do. I've only seen it shit." I nudged Penelope with my foot. She gave out a gusty sigh and slept on. "I appreciate your concern, Tommie."

"No, you don't."

"I just don't need it."

"Fine."

"You're shocked, that's all it is. She's an invalid. She's not the old Jane. It's been a few years since she was the old Jane. What did you expect?"

"I expected nothing." She started pacing the porch. "I don't know why I came. I'm sorry I came."

"Maybe you came to check up on our mortality and found it in place."

"Get off it."

"Maybe it reminds you of your own."

"It doesn't." She stood gazing out across the lawn towards the driveway. "She's in love with my son, Hal. This is disturbing to me."

I laughed. "Why shouldn't she be?"

"Because everyone is."

"He does a lot for her."

"I wish you'd all let him grow up, that's all. Frank's bad, but you're worse. Let go of him. The boy needs a life."

She turned and headed into the house and I said, "Always the last word." The dog got up and walked over to her, dragging its leash, and together they went inside.

For supper we had too much white wine, a Caesar salad, and the *bacalhau,* which was a disappointment. It was too salty and fishy, which it shouldn't have been. Cod is not a fishy fish. Tommie ate almost nothing. Brighton, helping himself to more of everything, said, "Mom, you've got to eat more. You're too skinny." She laughed, and he looked at her in surprise. "I'm not kidding."

"No, you're not. I know that." She laughed again.

"What's so funny? Don't you think you're thin? You are."

"Your mother was made thin," I said.

"Not this thin," said Brighton.

"Let's not discuss it," said Tommie. "It's like asking a lady her age, Bright. We don't."

He sat down and said to me, "Jane remembered her. Isn't that cool?"

I was surprised, but I said, "Of course she did."

"Of course she did, bullshit," said Tommie. "Who knows if she remembered me, and why should she? An appropriate look of terror crossed her face. Is that remembering?"

"It wasn't terror," said Brighton.

"It was close to it."

"Mom. She smiled."

Tommie looked at him. "I could wring your neck sometimes for being so sincere, you know that?"

He looked stricken and I said, "She was very fond of you, Tommie."

"Well, isn't that nice."

"You were the one I'd marry."

"Stop sticking your neck out, Hal."

"Want to wring mine too, Mrs. Haas? Here it is."

"Oh, shut up, both of you."

"Mom," said Brighton. He got up to clear the table. "Just cool it, okay? How's your headache?"

"What headache?"

"Before supper you said you had a splitting headache."

She shrugged. "I can't keep track of them."

"If I don't eat, sometimes I get a headache."

"If I don't drink, I do." He took a load out to the kitchen and she said to me, "He's a nice kid."

"Yes, he is."

"A babe."

"What do you mean?"

"An innocent."

"I don't know about that."

"Asexual."

"No."

"Why no?"

"Very few people are, that's all, and he's not one of them."

"I don't mean technically. I know all about the technical part, thank you. I mean emotionally. Helen is."

"Oh, come on. She's taking her time. Why are you in such a hurry? Don't say grandchildren."

Brighton came in again and Tommie said, "What about grandchildren, Bright? We're talking about you."

"You're strange, Mom."

"Why am I strange?"

"You know why you are."

"Tell me. I want to hear it from you. Why am I strange? Tell us why Mom's strange. Come on."

He had the good sense to turn his back on her. We moved into the living room and he brought in the coffee. Tommie said she'd like a drink. I got up to pour her another glass of wine. "A drink, Hal." She turned to Brighton. "Your friend here doesn't know what a drink is."

"Mom."

"You're bunking with a funny man, lovey."

"I made some coffee."

"I don't drink coffee, never have. Now get me something with gin in it." He didn't move. "With gin in it, please," she said.

"I can't, Mom."

"You can't, Mom? What's the long face?"

"There's wine. Just drink that. Can't you just drink that?"

"Can't you just drink that? You sound like a two-year-old. Whine, whine, whine." She shook her head sadly. "I didn't know you didn't approve. Is this new? Who's corrupted you? No, I don't care who's corrupted you. I really don't give a damn." She stood up. "Just show me where the liquor lives and I'll arrange my own destiny. I'll mix my own hemlock. Come on, Bright-Bright. Be a chump."

I am aware that as the disease progresses, only tiny amounts of alcohol are needed to produce a literally staggering drunkenness. I hadn't been around booze and Tommie together for a long time. My first reaction was pity, an unsettling, disorganized pity. My second was fear for us all. I said, "Tommie, that's enough. There's nothing in this house. You've had enough." I stood up next to her, prepared to block her search if necessary.

What I felt, standing there, terrified me. She was a machine. She had a machine's strength and nothing would stop her. I also knew she could read my mind. She looked me in the eye and laughed.

"Don't be stupid, Hal. Don't play stupid, baby games. I'll find it."

She left the room and Brighton said, "I think she's on some kind of medication."

I looked at him. "Are you kidding? She's drunk."

"No, I mean for the seizures. She's on some drug. She's not meant to drink when she's on it."

"Well, thanks, pal. This is a hell of a time to tell me. Why didn't you stop the wine at dinner?"

"I didn't think it would hurt."

"Hurt? I guess you don't know anything about drunks."

"Don't call her that."

"What am I to call her, my friend? Thirsty?"

"She drinks, that's all."

"Yes, she drinks. Finis," I said.

Tommie came back, holding a glass of clear liquid. She looked at me, smiling. "A toast to clarity," she said, and raised her hand. "Oh, spoilsports. Go to bed, both of you. My daughter Helen is the same way. Was. Such a heavy load of disapproval. Where is she, Brighton? Where is Helen today?"

"I don't know. I guess in California."

"On the nation's birthday?"

"I don't know."

"Let's call her up. Say happy birthday. Say hip hip to you. Shall we? Let's." She went and sat down on the sofa. She put her bare feet up on it and lay back against the pillows. "Call her. Oh, for God's sake. Bring me the phone and I'll call her."

"We're not calling her, Mom. Leave her alone. She's asleep."

"Bully," said Tommie. "Bully for her."

I said I was going to bed and she said, "It's seven p.m. in California. Don't be ridiculous."

"I'm in Connecticut," I said. "Goodnight, Tommie."

"Take my son with you." She laughed. "Go perform your unnatural acts together. Go on."

"Shut up, Mom."

She laughed again. "That got you, didn't it? They are unnatural, Bright-Bright. That's what makes them so glorious. Fucking is fun when it's illegal. Don't you think I know?" I watched her stare Brighton down. "I know."

"Go to bed," he said. "Just go to bed, Mom. Please. Please go to bed."

"He begs me. He calls me Mom." She threw her head back and put her hand to her chest. "I will sleep when I'm hungry, my son. What more can I promise? Maybe I'll go in and shoot the shit with Jane."

Brighton whispered to me, "What if she does?"

"Secrets?" said Tommie.

"Jane might be good for her," I said.

"She had a woman lover, as I remember," said Tommie.

"You remember wrong," I said.

"Oh, Hal. What a stupid bag of opinions you've become. What a remote figure. You used to vibrate with life. What happened? Too many young lovers? Tired of locking them in at night? Or is it your housemate here? Boy-o. Bright-Bright. Maybe you're tired of playing daddy to the whole wide world. Maybe you need to play with someone your own age."

"Goodnight, Tommie."

"Like me. Someone deader than thou. Maybe you need to be courted — courted, Hal. Imagine that. By someone courting death. That's what this is, isn't it? This whole rheumatic procedure? A long courtship. One fucking long hideous courtship unto death."

"So be it, Tommie," I said.

"Don't get biblical on me." She closed her eyes. As we left, she said, "Shut the door so I don't have to hear it." I can only guess it was an allusion to sex.

Sometime that night, protected by saints and angels, she got in her car and drove safely back to Vermont.

Helen

We had a sister, a little girl between us who died on the day she was born. Her name was Faith. As a child, when I thought of her, I never thought of a human being. I couldn't describe her in human terms, could not entrap her in a human form. That was her great beauty and usefulness. She could at any time be anything. The corner of my room that harbored the gorilla at night — I could turn that shadow into Faith. Or the chlorine blue above me, big as the sky and just as far away as I kicked my way to the surface of Hal's swimming pool, my chest exploding for lack of air — I'd call on Faith. I'd call *it* Faith. Whatever troubled or eluded me physically or mentally, came closer and allied itself with me in the word Faith.

But as I grew up, Faith became someone rather than something. She became a person whose absence I could account for only with death. She had been away too long for it to be otherwise. I once heard Tommie say she had lost a child, but "lost" did not describe her to my satisfaction. It implied she'd wandered away — or flown — and she had not. I went from feeling I had an explanation for all things and a guarantee of help whenever I needed it, to understanding that Faith was not a force greater than me, but a weaker human being who died. I didn't trouble myself with whether the dead could help the living. I knew they could not. Faith failed me in a way no one else ever had.

I was thirteen years old before I thought to bury her. I asked Brighton if he knew what happened to Faith and he said, "No. You mean how she died? No."

"I mean where she is. Where's her body?"

"Oh." He shook his head. "I never think about stuff like that. I don't think about her that way. Ask Mom."

I asked Tommie and she said, "I'll take you there." She drove me out the back way towards Morristown, a drive I liked. It had snowed the night before and the fields were holding the cover. It was late for snow, and I knew it wouldn't last long. We were in Dad's Volvo. Suddenly Tommie rolled her window down and I rolled mine down too. We both laughed. We had coats on and the wind felt good and clean and the snow seemed to bristle under the sun.

She pulled into a dirt road I'd noticed before. We bumped down it a short way to its end. The gravestones came right up to the road and I wondered if we were driving over anybody's feet. The cemetery was small and crowded, surrounded by trees. Many of the old stones tilted sideways and some had fallen over on their faces. I asked Tommie why they all fell the same way when they fell, and she said she thought it might have to do with the slope of the land which didn't seem sloped to me.

Faith was in a corner in the shade. I pulled my coat around me. I asked Tommie if I was stepping on her body and she said no. I said, "How do you know?"

"Because she's in a jar, Helen."

"She's in a jar?"

"An urn. She's cremated. She's ashes in an urn."

I had never thought of this possibility for my sister before, and my hands went to my face. Tommie said, "She's all here, sweetie. There's nothing missing." It was meant to comfort me, but it was a funny thing to say. It was a way of saying that death is not an unknown, is kinder than the unknown, and life is very physical for all the other things it is.

On our way home we stopped at a Dairy Queen and ate our ice cream looking out over a field from which the snow was disappearing in long stripes. I asked Tommie if a baby's bones are soft and she said they were, that they had to be in order to travel. I said I was glad we went and she said she was too. I asked if we would all be there where Faith was, and she said there was room for all of us.

I don't work as much as I used to. I go to work when I'm ready and come home when everyone else does. In the morning I take my cup of coffee to the armchair and sit and write about my life. I write about my family. The things I remember surprise me as much as the things I've forgotten. I'm discovering that no one thing holds all the glory, nor therefore all the blame. I'm discovering that love, as much as hate, is a conspiracy. It requires intention, and in some cases effort. In a family, in our family, I always thought the adults' job was to love the kids. In different ways. With food, with a house, with furniture and privacy. With things. I didn't think about love as an emotion.

Anger was an emotion. So was bitterness. At a certain point in our lives, everything Tommie did was emotional. But none of it that I could understand had to do with love.

I know now that she was sick. After the car wreck her brain was doing strange things. She was physically in danger, and she endangered herself more by getting drunk sometimes, or anyway, drinking. This is a part of her life I would like to know nothing about, but I know it all. I would like to reach in and extract that unhappiness, that bitterness right at her core. I would like to save her life, put her back on track, take booze away, take memory away if necessary. I would like to have her back again and I can't. Not the old Tommie. Not the old Helen either. Not the old anyone. The movement is forward not back. When I write about the people we used to be, I do it to move forward. The more I write, the less I want to stay in those old places. The more I write, the more I see what a sad and lonely kid I was, who grew up into a sad and lonely teenager, who grew up into a sad and lonely adult. I had a feeling all along there was a crazy kind of point system, the most unfair game you can think of, where one false move could wreck your whole life. I saw Tommie's life go to pieces and I figured we were on the same ride. There was no sense to that. Sense isn't mostly what we react with. She and I have always been too close for our own good, even when we couldn't stand each other. Even when we were miles apart, time and the whole country between us. I'd still find her. I'd find people just like her. There was no running from her. That's why I finally went home.

Maria DiAngelo taught me how to fight. She said, "Elbows, knees, hands, feet — all good weapons, Helen. But the best weapon you have is your mind."

I was quick. I was a quick learner. My movements were fast,

and as she said, like an animal. Instinctive. Coming from the center of my body. That's why people who do karate can be everywhere at once. They know where the center of the body is, and in their mind they stay there. They never leave it. They can kick the ceiling and not even leave the floor. Watching Maria fight, she looked rested. I never got as far as that, or even close.

She taught me not to fight, ever, physically, unless I had to, and if I had to, I must move forward, contact, engage, and never hold back. Never retreat. Retreat leaves the body open and vulnerable. I must do damage at close range, with all my body's weapons. Move in, move in, move towards. Into the center of that other body. The intimacy is unexpected, unnerving, and powerful.

When I broke my arm, it strengthened my mind. Every time I've hurt my body, my mind has become stronger and clearer. When you set the body aside, you eliminate a great distraction. The monkey, as Maria called it. There was the monkey body, and the monkey mind. They were like energetic children, racing back and forth and around in circles to exhaustion. When I was fifteen I worshipped exhaustion. It was the only untroubled state I knew. To be exhausted and fall into bed and sleep. Those were the good moments of life.

Maria said, "That's ridiculous. That's how people get on drugs. They want to blank out."

I was one-armed then and she was showing me how to fight with my mind, how to mentally repel people. How to use all my intention to say no, get away from me, without saying a word. Without moving. Just the eyes. Everything came into focus. The effort was incredible, as if I were actually exercising some physical part of my body. At the end of an hour I'd feel something like exhaustion, but not exhaustion. An energetic stillness. Maria said, "I think what you're feeling is calm."

"Calm? Huh."

"Does it feel kind of peaceful?"

"It feels kind of nothing. Yeah, kind of peaceful."

"That's calm."

It was difficult — no, impossible — to take this good feeling home with me, for which I resented home and everyone in it. Years later, now, I am unpracticed, slow, hardly an animal, hardly an athlete anymore, and yet I feel like I have fought the battle of my life, and won it. It had to do with Tommie. It involved getting on a bus, letting Hal put me on the bus in New York City. Letting him pack a lunch for me, a peanut butter sandwich and an apple. I said, "Bye, I'm off to kindergarten," meaning a lunch like that. He was very serious. He said, "No, Helen. This is all new. This is a place you've never been before. You're good. This is good what you're doing. You're very brave." Then he said, "I love you," and started to cry.

All the way up on the bus I tried not to think about what I was going to, because every time I thought about it I got scared. Brighton wanted to lend me a book for the trip, but I said no, I couldn't read books on buses, maybe I'd get a magazine. There was an old *New York Times* jammed between the seats and I read some of that, but mostly I just sat and watched the side of the highway go by, and for a while I slept.

Tommie met me and took me to a place across the street from the bus station, an old railroad car turned into a diner. I had coffee and she had hot tea. At first she looked almost the same. Her face was thinner, and there was something the matter with her right eye, it kept twitching. She said I looked very different. She didn't ask if I was hungry. She didn't say I looked too thin. I was grateful for that. We didn't try and come up with things to talk about. I don't know what we talked about. She was wearing a terrible pair of houndstooth slacks and a tan turtleneck, slack in the neck and dirty. Over that a red plaid hunter's jacket.

"This will be a pretty short visit," I told her.

She looked out the window. I did too. A view of the diner parking lot. Beyond that a row of young trees planted along the sidewalk, and across the street a dark, stone building that looked like a bank.

"Everyone's been really nice to me," I said. "Dad is like this changed person."

"He wants me to live with him again."

"You're kidding. He didn't tell me that."

"No? I'm not surprised."

"I am. We talked about you a lot."

"I'm sure you did. Everyone does. It's morbid."

"Mom, he can talk now. He didn't used to be able to talk."

"You don't have to sing his praises. I know your father. I like him. If he were a pathetic character, I could be a cruel mate. But he isn't, and I'm not. You don't need to worry about him or protect him. I did that for years. That's why it's taken him this long to talk and cook."

"So now you go live with him. That's good. I think that's great."

"Don't assume I said yes." She shifted to face the window, reached out and put her hand on the glass. Something to look at, something to study. "I said we'll see."

"We'll see? You really like it here?"

"No. Not particularly. I wasn't cut out for this kind of life. I don't have the right clothes. I hate being cold. I hate vegetables. I don't even like gardens. I'm not a strapping gal."

"You look tired. You look pretty worn out."

"Thank you."

"What do they make you do here?"

"Nothing. You do what you can do."

"Like what?"

"Like what everyone else does who lives in a family, unless they're spoiled, which you were. We all were."

"Who spoiled us?"

"Money spoiled you. Money and circumstance."

"Don't blame money."

"I will blame money. I'll blame whatever I want."

"You're the spoiled one. Why don't you stop playing destitute and get some clothes? If you're going to live here, live here. Take care of yourself. Buy some warm clothes. Buy yourself a heater. Get that eye checked out."

She looked at me blankly.

"That eye on your face. The one in constant motion." She touched her right eye and I said, "Yes. That one. It's just neglect, Mom."

"You came to bully me."

"I didn't. I came to see you."

"Well, see me then, goddammit," she hissed. She yanked her body around in her seat so she was facing me. Bit her lip with what seemed like a spasm of pain. "You can't keep twisting the knife. It's too easy, Helen. Others will turn against you. This is the point in the play where the old woman turns on herself, and the weak move towards her, while the decent move away."

"I moved away. I moved far away."

"Yes, you did. Did it change anything?"

"Yes! I mean, yes. It gave me some room. It gave me some time to think."

"Why the sudden need to come back?" She leaned forward. Metallic breath. Hint of lemon from the tea. "You see, I struggle with that. There are days, plenty of them, when I want to run home, run to the known, to your father, run right back into that place I left and live there again. But to live there again I could only be the person I was, and I'm not that person."

"Dad's not the person he was, and he lives there."

"But he likes himself. I don't like myself. When I like myself, I'll go home."

"How long are you planning to live, Mom?"

She smiled. "I might live out the day." She covered her eye, which was fluttering like crazy. Shrugged. "Might not."

"I like myself, too," I said. "I don't want to run home. I'm not running home. That's not what this is. I like where I live. It's okay there. I'm okay there."

"I'm impressed, Helen."

"I don't know if you mean that or not."

"You came a long way to tell me." She put her hands on the table. Knuckles chapped, wrist bones protruding. An almost imperceptible tremor. "I admire you," she said. "That's something you never knew. The others were often gutless, but you. Not once. You were She-Who-Does-Not-Bow-To-Gods-Nor-Idols. You shunned me. They clung to me. You were all fire and backbone and you went your way. Maybe you thought it was me who made you who you are, but it never was. It was all you. You were always that way." She leaned back, closed her eyes, opened them again. "I think Faith sent you."

"Faith?"

"I've always thought that."

"Sent me where?"

"Here. To me."

"Why?"

"Because she saw my potential. She assessed the job and couldn't do it, and went back for you."

"Why me?"

"Because you're a fighter. She needed a fighter. I was a little ball of waxy light — that was my potential — surrounded by teeth and claws. I could be mean. I was scrappy. She wasn't scrappy. She was kind. She had a kind, carefree nature. You can tell all this about a newborn. It's the strangest thing. I knew she wouldn't live. The moment she arrived, I knew she was headed back. One look at me . . . " She smiled at her lap. "Kindness never was the way to my heart."

"Send in the Marines."

"Yes."

"You like being punished."

"It's true. I do."

"I can't do it anymore, Mom. Punish you."

"Oh, it's not you, Helen. It's never been you. It's me. I do it best myself."

I remembered something she once told me, or maybe she told Brighton and he told me. She said, in order to fight someone face to face, you have to care about them. Armor, she said, was to protect soldiers from their own compassion. Her armor, I saw, had distracted me from many things. It was well-made, and it fit her body well. It fit her so well I forgot it was there. The armor *was* Tommie. It had a darkness and a sharp edge to it, and a shine that attracted some and blinded others. I was blinded by it. So was Brighton. I only knew of two people who had succeeded in loving her, Dad and Hal, and they had loved the person inside the armor. They had loved Tommie. They had known her that long.

She was right, I was a fighter. I pushed her. Sometimes she pushed me back. But more often she didn't. I don't know what her feelings were about me. We went our own ways, fiercely at times, hurt at times, often lonely. When I needed to connect I fought her again.

I had come here to fight her, hadn't I? And who was she? A woman with a crazy eye, head floating on a thin neck, bony shoulders hunched to protect her flat, bony chest. Trembling hands, dirty nails. Filthy clothes, hanging on her like sacks. She was someone I no longer belonged to. I couldn't imagine coming out of her body. And yet we looked alike. I had her face. We were somehow alike. Under her armor she was someone who wanted to be seen. She wanted to be uncovered. By me. Maybe by others, too, but right now, today, by me. I knew I would never again need an enemy as I had needed Tommie to be my enemy. I had been in awe of her all my life.

I paid for our tea and coffee and we left the diner. She asked if I'd like to see where she lived and I said no, not this time. Maybe some other time.

"You wouldn't like it," she said. We crossed the street.

"I might. It's a farm, right?"

"A small farm."

"Brighton says you live in a teepee."

"A teepee! That's very romantic. Tell your brother it's an A-frame house."

"He says you have a dog."

"She's everyone's dog, but I'm the one she sleeps with. She's an old dog. Her name's Penelope."

"You live with women?"

"Five other women. The house down the road has some live-in boyfriends and kids."

"That's good. Kids help."

She pulled her jacket around her. Apparently the zipper didn't zip. "You can see your motel from here." She pointed past the bank. "Brighton stays there."

"That's what he said."

"You've got everything?"

"I'm all set."

"What time do you leave in the morning?"

"Early. I don't know what time exactly. Seven o'clock. Pretty early."

"I'm glad you're not driving. It's a long drive."

"I don't mind the bus. I kind of like it. I'll just sleep. And think."

We said good-bye in front of her car. No embrace. That was Tommie's way. It was almost dark. I wanted only to lie down on my motel bed and close my eyes. I hadn't eaten since Hal's peanut butter sandwich, and I realized I was hungry. I felt shaky with hunger. The motel had a coffee shop and I ordered a jelly omelet and a baked potato. Afterwards, a cup of hot chocolate.

That night my room faced the wall of the bank. This room faces a dear little grubby alley. I can hear dogs overturning trash cans day and night. Sometimes the smell of garlic is so strong I have to cook something of my own to feel like I live here. I put what's left of the coffee on to boil, a full boil, until the apartment no longer smells of Chinese breakfast. It smells of awakeness and aliveness.

I like it here. I have new lamps, standing lamps. The end tables are gone. Out on the street to furnish somebody else's hovel. I got Brighton a bed. He can sleep up off the floor now when he visits. Or I can if I have company. It's a double bed. It takes up most of the living room. I still like a twin bed when I sleep by myself. My own room and my own bed. In the morning, when I write, I sit in the armchair and put my feet on the new bed and feel it isn't wasted.

A NOTE ON THE AUTHOR

MARGARET ERHART is the author of two previous nov-
els, *Unusual Company* (1987) and *Augusta Cotton* (1992).
She lives in Truro, Massachusetts.

A NOTE ON THE BOOK

This book was composed by Steerforth Press using a digital
version of Garamond, a typeface originally designed by
Claude Garamond in the early sixteenth century, and re-
drawn by Robert Slimbach and issued by Adobe in 1989.
The book was printed on acid free papers and bound by
Quebecor Printing - Book Press Inc. of North Brattleboro,
Vermont.